PENGU

TALE

THE LITTLE WOR

Giovanni Guareschi lived at Parma, near the River Po, where he was born in 1908. His parents wished him to be a naval engineer: consequently he studied law, made a name as a sign-board painter, and, among other jobs, gave mandolin lessons. His father had a heavy black moustache under his nose: Giovanni grew one just like it. He always wore it and was proud of it. He was not bald, wrote eight books, and was five feet ten inches tall. 'I also have a brother,' Guareschi said, adding, 'but I prefer not to discuss him. And I have a motor-cycle with four cylinders, an automobile with six cylinders, and a wife and two children.'

As a young man he drew cartoons for *Bertoldo*. When the war came he was arrested by the political police for howling in the streets all one night. In 1943 he was captured by the Germans at Alessandria and adopted the slogan: 'I will not die even if they kill me.' Back in Italy after the war he became editor-in-chief of *Candido* at Milan, in which his famous *Don Camillo* stories first appeared. He scripted a film, *People Like This*. Giovanni Guareschi died in 1968.

Giovanni Guareschi

Tales from

Penguin Books

The Little World of

Don Camillo

Penguin Books Ltd, Harmondsworth, Middlesex, England
Penguin Books, 625 Madison Avenue, New York, New York 10022, U.S.A.
Penguin Books Australia Ltd, Ringwood, Victoria, Australia
Penguin Books Canada Ltd, 2801 John Street, Markham, Ontario, Canada L3R 1B4
Penguin Books (N.Z.) Ltd, 182–190 Wairau Road, Auckland 10, New Zealand

'How I Got Like This', 'The Little World', 'A Confession', 'A Baptism', 'Evening School', 'The Treasure', 'Crime and Punishment', 'Return to the Fold' and 'Nocturne with Bells' originally appeared in *The Little World of Don Camillo*
First published in Great Britain by Gollancz 1951

'Victims of War', 'A Speech to Go Down in History', 'Made in U.S.S.R.', 'Inflation in the Po Valley', 'Operation Saint Babila' and 'The New Look' originally appeared in *Don Camillo and the Devil*
First published in Great Britain by Gollancz 1957

'Peppone Goes Back to School', 'A Lesson in Tactics', 'Holiday Joys' and 'Back to 1922' originally appeared in *Don Camillo's Dilemma*
First published in Great Britain by Gollancz 1954

'The Stuff from America', 'A Matter of Conscience', 'The Prodigal Son', 'Thunder', 'Benefit of Clergy', 'Technique of the *Coup d'Etat*' originally appeared in *Don Camillo and the Prodigal Son*
First published in Great Britain by Gollancz 1952

'Gold Fever' was originally published in *Comrade Don Camillo*
First published in Italy as *Mondo Piccolo: Il Compagno Don Camillo* in 1963
First published in Great Britain by Gollancz 1964

All the stories in this selection were translated by Frances Frenaye, except for 'How I Got Like This', 'The Little World', 'A Confession', 'A Baptism', 'Evening School', 'The Treasure', 'Crime and Punishment', 'Return to the Fold' and 'Nocturne with Bells', which were translated by Una Vincenzo Troubridge.

Made and printed in Great Britain
by Richard Clay (The Chaucer Press) Ltd,
Bungay, Suffolk
Set in Linotype Baskerville

CONTENTS

1 · How I Got Like This · 9

2 · The Little World · 15

3 · A Confession · 17

4 · A Baptism · 22

5 · Evening School · 27

6 · The Treasure · 31

7 · Nocturne with Bells · 40

8 · Victims of War · 45

9 · A Speech to Go Down in History · 54

10 · Peppone Goes Back to School · 62

11 · The Stuff from America · 77

12 · A Matter of Conscience · 84

13 · Made in U.S.S.R. · 90

14 · Inflation in the Po Valley · 100

15 · Gold Fever · 108

16 · A Lesson in Tactics · 119

17 · Crime and Punishment · 132

18 · Return to the Fold · 141

19 · The Prodigal Son · 150

20 · Thunder · 156

21 · Operation Saint Babila · 168

22 · The New Look · 177

23 · Benefit of Clergy · 183

24 · Holiday Joys · 191

25 · Technique of the *Coup d'État* · 202

26 · Back to 1922 · 210

TALES FROM
THE LITTLE WORLD OF
DON CAMILLO

1 · HOW I GOT LIKE THIS

My life began on the 1st of May 1908, and between one thing and another, it still goes on.

When I was born my mother had been teaching in the elementary school for nine years and she continued to teach until the end of 1949. In recognition of her work, the parish priest of the village presented her with an alarm clock in the name of all the people, and after fifty years of teaching in schools where there was no electric light or water but, in compensation, an abundant supply of cockroaches, flies, and mosquitoes, my mother now passes her time waiting for the State to consider her request for a pension and listening to the tick-tock of the alarm clock given her by the village.

At the time when I was born my father was interested in all kinds of machines, from harvesters to gramophones, and he possessed an enormous moustache, very similar to the one I wear under my nose. He still has the splendid moustache, but for some time he has not been interested in much of anything, and he passes his time reading the newspapers. He also reads what I write, but he does not like my way of writing and thinking.

In his day my father was a very brilliant man, and he travelled around by automobile at a time, in Italy, when entire populations went from one town to another in order to see that darned machine that ran by itself. The only memory I have of these ancient splendours is an old automobile horn – the kind with the rubber ball that you squeeze. My father screwed this to the head of his bed and he used to sound it every so often, especially in the summertime.

I also have a brother, but I had an argument with him two weeks ago and I prefer not to discuss him.

In addition to the above I have a motor-cycle with four cylinders, an automobile with six cylinders, and a wife and two children.

My parents had decided that I should become a naval engineer and so I ended up studying law and thus, in a short time, I became famous as a signboard artist and caricaturist. Since no one at school had ever made me study drawing, drawing naturally had a particular fascination for me and, after doing caricatures and public advertisements, I studied wood-carving and scenic design.

At the same time I kept busy as a doorman in a sugar refinery, a superintendent of a parking lot for bicycles, and since I knew nothing at all about music I began to give mandolin lessons to some friends. I had an excellent record as a census-taker. I was a teacher in a boarding-school and then I got a job correcting proofs on a local newspaper. To supplement my modest salary I began to write stories about local events and since I had a free day on Sunday I took over the editorship of the weekly magazine which came out on Monday. In order to get it together as quickly as possible I wrote three-quarters of it.

One fine day I took a train and went to Milan, where I wormed my way into a humour magazine called *Bertoldo.* Here I was forced to stop writing, but I was allowed to draw. I took advantage of this by drawing in white on black paper, something which created vast depressed areas in the magazine.

I was born in Parma near the Po River; people born in this area have heads as hard as pig iron and I succeeded in becoming editor-in-chief of *Bertoldo.* This is the magazine in which Saul Steinberg, who at that time was studying architecture in Milan, published his first drawings and for which he worked until he left to go to America.

For reasons entirely beyond my control, the war broke out and one day in 1942 I went on a terrific drunk because my brother was lost in Russia and I couldn't find out anything about him. That night I went up and down the streets of Milan shouting things which filled several sheets of legal-size paper – as I found out the next day when I was arrested by the political police. Then a lot of people worried about me and they finally got me released. However, the political police wanted me out of circulation and so had me called into the army, and on the 9th of September 1943, with the fall of Fascism, I was taken prisoner again, this time at Alessandria in Northern Italy by the Germans. Since I did not want to work for the Germans, I was sent to a Polish concentration camp. I was in various German concentration camps until April 1945, when my camp was taken over by the English and after five months I was sent back to Italy.

The period I spent in prison was the most intensely active of my life. In fact I had to do everything to stay alive and succeeded almost completely by dedicating myself to a precise programme which is summarized in my slogan 'I will not die even if they kill me.' (It is not easy to remain alive when one is reduced to a sack of bones of which the total weight is one hundred pounds, and this includes lice, bedbugs, fleas, hunger, and melancholy.)

When I returned to Italy I found that many things were changed, especially the Italians, and I spent a good deal of time trying to figure out whether they had changed for the better or for the worse. In the end I discovered that they had not changed at all, and then I became so depressed that I shut myself in my house.

Shortly afterwards a new magazine called *Candido* was established in Milan and, in working for it, I found myself up to my eyes in politics, although I was then, and still am, an independent. Nevertheless, the magazine values my contributions very highly – perhaps because I am editor-in-chief.

A few months ago the leader of the Italian Communists, Mr Palmiro Togliatti, made a speech in which he lost his temper and called the Milanese journalist who invented the character with the triple nostrils 'a triple idiot'. The threefold idiot is me and this was for me the most prized recognition of my work as a political journalist. The man with three nostrils is now famous in Italy, and it was I who created him. I must admit that I am proud because to succeed in characterizing a Communist with a stroke of the pen (that is, putting under the nose three, instead of two, nostrils) is not a bad idea, and it worked very well.

And why should I be modest? The other things that I wrote and drew during the days before the election also worked very well; to prove it I have in my attic a sack full of newspaper clippings which malign me; whoever wants to know more can come and read them.

The stories in *The Little World of Don Camillo* were very successful in Italy, and this book, which collects the first series of these stories, is already in its seventh edition. Many people have written long articles on *The Little World of Don Camillo* and many people have written me letters about this or that story, and so now I am a little confused, and I would find myself rather embarrassed if I had to make any judgement of *The Little World of Don Camillo*. The background of these stories is my home, Parma, the Emilian Plain along the Po where political passion often reaches a disturbing intensity, and yet these people are attractive and hospitable and generous and have a highly developed sense of humour. It must be the sun, a terrible sun which beats on their brains during the summer, or perhaps it is the fog, a heavy fog, which oppresses them during the winter.

The people in these stories are true to life and the stories are so true that more than once, after I had written a story, the thing actually happened and one read it in the news.

In fact the truth surpasses the imagination. I once wrote a story about the Communist, Peppone, who was annoyed during a political meeting by an aeroplane which threw down pamphlets of the opposition. Peppone took up a machine-gun, but he could not bring himself to fire on the plane. When I wrote this I said to myself, 'This is too fantastic.' Some months later at Spilimberg not ony did the Communists fire on an aeroplane that distributed anti-Communist pamphlets, but they shot it down.

I have nothing more to say about *The Little World of Don Camillo*. You can't expect that after a poor fellow has written a book he should also understand it.

I am 5 feet 10 inches high and I have written eight books in all. I have also done a movie which is called *People Like This,* now being distributed throughout Italy. Many people like the movie; others do not like it. As far as I am concerned, the movie leaves me indifferent. Many things in life leave me indifferent now, but that is not my fault. It is the fault of the war. The war destroyed a lot of things we had within us. We have seen too many dead and too many living. In addition to 5 feet 10 inches, I have all my hair.

G. G.

2 · THE LITTLE WORLD

THE Little World of Don Camillo is to be found somewhere in the valley of the Po River. It is almost any village on that stretch of plain in Northern Italy. There, between the Po and the Apennines, the climate is always the same. The landscape never changes and, in country like this, you can stop along any road for a moment and look at a farmhouse sitting in the midst of maize and hemp – and immediately a story is born.

Why do I tell you this instead of getting on with my story? Because I want you to understand that, in the Little World between the river and the mountains, many things can happen that cannot happen anywhere else. Here, the deep, eternal breathing of the river freshens the air, for both the living and the dead, and even the dogs have souls If you keep this in mind, you will easily come to know the village priest, Don Camillo, and his adversary, Peppone, the Communist Mayor. You will not be surprised that Christ watches the goings-on from a big cross in the village church and not infrequently talks, and that one man beats the other over the head, but fairly – that is, without hatred – and that in the end the two enemies find they agree about essentials.

And one final word of explanation before I begin my story. If there is a priest anywhere who feels offended by my treatment of Don Camillo, he is welcome to break the biggest candle available over my head. And if there is a Communist who feels offended by Peppone, he is welcome to break a hammer and sickle on my back. But if there is anyone who is offended by the conversations of Christ, I can't help it; for the one who speaks in this story is not Christ, but my Christ – that is, the voice of my conscience.

3 · A CONFESSION

DON CAMILLO had been born with a constitutional preference for calling a spade a spade. Upon a certain occasion when there had been a local scandal involving landowners of ripe age and young girls of his parish, he had, in the course of his mass, embarked upon a seemly and suitably generalized address, when he had suddenly become aware of the fact that one of the chief offenders was present among the foremost ranks of his congregation. Flinging all restraint to the four winds and also flinging a hastily snatched cloth over the head of the Crucified Lord above the high altar in order that the divine ears might not be offended, he had set his arms firmly akimbo and had resumed his sermon. And so stentorian had been the voice that issued from the lips of the big man and so uncompromising had been his language that the very roof of the little church had seemed to tremble.

When the time of the elections drew near Don Camillo had naturally been explicit in his allusions to the local leftists. Thus there came a fine evening when, as he was going home at dusk, an individual muffled in a cloak sprang out of a hedge as he passed by and, taking advantage of the fact that Don Camillo was handicapped by his bicycle and by a large parcel containing seventy eggs attached to its handlebars, belaboured him with a heavy stick and promptly vanished as though the earth had swallowed him.

Don Camillo had kept his own counsel. Having arrived at the presbytery and deposited the eggs in safety, he had gone into the church to discuss the matter with the Lord, as was his invariable habit in moments of perplexity.

'What should I do?' Don Camillo had inquired.

'Anoint your back with a little oil beaten up in water and hold your tongue,' the Lord had replied from above the altar. 'We must forgive those who offend us. That is the rule.'

'Very true, Lord,' agreed Don Camillo, 'but on this occasion we are discussing blows, not offences.'

'And what do you mean by that? Surely you are not trying to tell me that injuries done to the body are more painful than those aimed at the spirit?'

'I see your point, Lord. But You should also bear in mind that in the beating of me, who am Your minister, an injury has been done to Yourself also. I am really more concerned on Your behalf than on my own.'

'And was I not a greater minister of God than you

are? And did I not forgive those who nailed me to the Cross?'

'There is never any use arguing with You!' Don Camillo had exclaimed. 'You are always in the right. Your will be done. We must forgive. All the same, don't forget that if these ruffians, encouraged by my silence, should crack my skull, the responsibility will lie with You. I could cite several passages from the Old Testament ...'

'Don Camillo, are you proposing to instruct me in the Old Testament? As for this business, I assume full responsibility. Moreover, strictly between Ourselves, the beating has done you no harm. It may teach you to let politics alone in my house.'

Don Camillo had duly forgiven. But nevertheless one thing had stuck in his gullet like a fish bone: curiosity as to the identity of his assailant.

Time passed. Late one evening, while he sat in the confessional, Don Camillo discerned through the grille the countenance of the local leader of the extreme leftists, Peppone.

That Peppone should come to confession at all was a sensational event, and Don Camillo was proportionately gratified.

'God be with you, brother; with you who, more than any other man, have need of His holy blessing. It is a long time since you last went to confession?'

'Not since 1918,' replied Peppone.

'You must have committed a great number of sins in the course of those twenty-eight years, with your head so crammed with crazy notions ...'

'A good few, undoubtedly,' sighed Peppone.

'For example?'

'For example, two months ago I gave you a hiding.'

'That was serious indeed,' replied Don Camillo, 'since in assaulting a minister of God, you have attacked God Himself.'

'But I have repented,' exclaimed Peppone. 'And, moreover, it was not as God's minister that I beat you, but as my political adversary. In any case, I did it in a moment of weakness.'

'Apart from this and from your membership of your accursed Party, have you any other grave sins on your conscience?'

Peppone spilled all the beans.

Taken as a whole, his offences were not very serious, and Don Camillo let him off with a score of Paters and Aves. Then, while Peppone was kneeling at the altar rails performing his penance, Don Camillo went and knelt before the crucifix.

'Lord,' he said, 'You must forgive me, but I am going to beat him up for You.'

'You are going to do nothing of the kind,' replied the Lord. 'I have forgiven him and you must forgive him also. All things considered, he is not a bad soul.'

'Lord, you can never trust a Red! They live by lies. Only look at him; Barabbas incarnate!'

'It's as good a face as most, Don Camillo; it is your heart that is venomous!'

'Lord, if I have ever served You well, grant me just one small grace: let me at least break this candle on his shoulders. Dear Lord, what, after all, is a candle?'

'No,' replied the Lord. 'Your hands were made for blessing, not for striking.'

Don Camillo sighed heavily.

He genuflected and left the sanctuary. As he turned to make a final sign of the cross he found himself exactly behind Peppone who, on his knees, was apparently absorbed in prayer.

'Lord,' groaned Don Camillo, clasping his hands and gazing at the crucifix. 'My hands were made for blessing, but not my feet!'

'There is something in that,' replied the Lord from

above the altar, 'but all the same, Don Camillo, bear it in mind: only one!'

The kick landed like a thunderbolt and Peppone received it without so much as blinking an eye. Then he got to his feet and sighed with relief.

'I've been waiting for that for the last ten minutes,' he remarked. 'I feel better now.'

'So do I!' exclaimed Don Camillo, whose heart was now as light and serene as a May morning.

The Lord said nothing at all, but it was easy enough to see that He too was pleased.

4 · A BAPTISM

ONE day the church was unexpectedly invaded by a man and two women, one of whom was Peppone's wife.

Don Camillo, who from the top of a pair of steps was cleaning St Joseph's halo with Brasso, turned round and inquired what they wanted.

'There is something here that needs to be baptized,' replied the man, and one of the women held up a bundle containing a baby.

'Whose is it?' inquired Don Camillo, coming down from his steps.

'Mine,' replied Peppone's wife.

'And your husband's?' persisted Don Camillo.

'Well, naturally! Who else do you suppose gave it to me?' retorted Peppone's wife indignantly.

'No need to be offended,' observed Don Camillo on his way to the sacristy. 'Haven't I been told often enough that your Party approves of free love?'

As he passed before the high altar Don Camillo knelt down and permitted himself a discreet wink in the direction of the Lord. 'Did you hear that one?' he murmured with a joyful grin. 'One in the eye for the Godless ones!'

'Don't talk rubbish, Don Camillo,' replied the Lord irritably. 'If they had no God, why should they come here to get their child baptized? If Peppone's wife had boxed your ears it would only have served you right.'

'If Peppone's wife had boxed my ears I should have taken the three of them by the scruff of their necks and . . .'

'And what?' inquired the Lord severely.

'Oh, nothing; just a figure of speech,' Don Camillo hastened to assure Him, rising to his feet.

'Don Camillo, watch your step,' said the Lord sternly.

Duly vested, Don Camillo approached the font. 'What do you wish to name this child?' he asked Peppone's wife.

'Lenin Libero Antonio,' she replied.

'Then go and get him baptized in Russia,' said Don Camillo calmly, replacing the cover on the font.

The priest's hands were as large as shovels and the three left the church without protest. But as Don Camillo was attempting to slip into the sacristy he was arrested by the voice of the Lord.

'Don Camillo, you have done a very wicked thing. Go at once and bring those people back and baptize their child.'

'But, Lord,' protested Don Camillo, 'You really must

bear in mind that baptism is not a jest. Baptism is a very sacred matter. Baptism is ...'

'Don Camillo,' the Lord interrupted him. 'Are you attempting to teach me the nature of baptism? Did I not invent it? I tell you that you have been guilty of gross presumption, because, suppose that child were to die at this moment, it would be your fault if it failed to attain Paradise!'

'Lord, do not let us be melodramatic,' retorted Don Camillo. 'Why in the name of Heaven should it die? It's as pink and white as a rose!'

'Which means exactly nothing!' the Lord admonished him. 'What if a tile should fall on its head or it should suddenly have convulsions? It was your duty to baptize it.'

Don Camillo raised protesting arms: 'But Lord, just think it over. If it were certain that the child would go to Hell, we might stretch a point; but seeing that despite being the son of that nasty piece of work he might very easily manage to slip into Paradise, how can You ask me to risk anyone going there with such a name as Lenin? I'm thinking of the reputation of Paradise.'

'The reputation of Paradise is my business,' shouted the Lord angrily. 'What matters to me is that a man should be a decent fellow and I care less than nothing whether his name be Lenin or Button. At the very most, you should have pointed out to those people that saddling children with fantastic names may involve them in annoyances when they grow up.'

'Very well,' replied Don Camillo. 'I am always in the wrong. I must see what I can do about it.'

Just at that moment someone came into the church. It was Peppone, alone, with the baby in his arms. He closed the church door and bolted it.

'I do not leave this church,' he said, 'until my son has been baptized with the name that I have chosen.'

'Look at that,' whispered Don Camillo, smiling as

he turned towards the Lord. 'Now do You see what these people are? One is filled with the holiest intentions and this is how they treat you.'

'Put yourself in his place,' replied the Lord. 'One may not approve his attitude, but one can understand it.'

Don Camillo shook his head.

'I have already said that I do not leave this place unless you baptize my son as I demand!' repeated Peppone. Whereupon, laying the bundle containing the baby upon a bench, he took off his coat, rolled up his sleeves, and advanced threateningly.

'Lord,' implored Don Camillo. 'I ask You! If You think it just that one of your priests should give way to the threats of a layman, then I must obey. But in that event, if tomorrow they should bring me a calf and compel me to baptize it You must not complain. You know very well how dangerous it is to create precedents.'

'All right,' replied the Lord, 'but in this case you must try to make him understand ...'

'And if he hits me?'

'Then you must accept it. You must endure and suffer as I did.'

Don Camillo turned to his visitor. 'Very well, Peppone,' he said. 'The baby will leave the church baptized, but not by that accursed name.'

'Don Camillo,' stuttered Peppone, 'don't forget that my stomach has never recovered from the bullet that I stopped in the mountains. If you hit low, I shall go for you with a bench.'

'Don't worry, Peppone. I can deal with you entirely in the upper storeys,' Don Camillo assured him, landing him a neat one above the ear.

They were both burly men with muscles of steel, and their blows fairly whistled through the air. After twenty minutes of silent and furious combat, Don

Camillo distinctly heard a voice behind him. 'Now, Don Camillo! The point of the jaw!' It came from the Lord above the altar. Don Camillo struck hard and Peppone crashed to the ground.

He remained where he lay for some ten minutes; then he sat up, got to his feet, rubbed his jaw, shook himself, put on his jacket, and reknotted his red handkerchief. Then he picked up the baby. Fully vested, Don Camillo was waiting for him, steady as a rock, beside the font. Peppone approached him slowly.

'What am I to name him?' asked Don Camillo.

'Camillo Libero Antonio,' muttered Peppone.

Don Camillo shook his head. 'No; we will name him Libero Camillo Lenin,' he said. 'Yes, Lenin. When you have a Camillo around, such folk as he are quite helpless.'

'Amen,' muttered Peppone, gently prodding his jaw.

When all was done and Don Camillo passed before the altar and the Lord smiled and remarked: 'Don Camillo, I am bound to admit that in politics you are My master.'

'And also in fisticuffs,' replied Don Camillo with perfect gravity, carelessly fingering a large lump on his forehead.

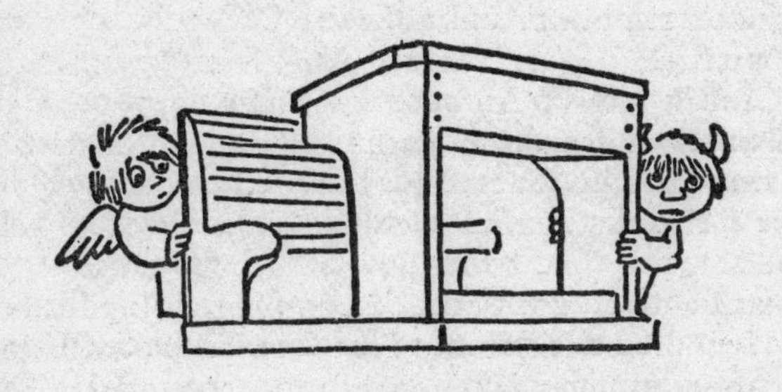

5 · EVENING SCHOOL

In the empty church, by the faint light of the two altar candles, Don Camillo was chatting with the Lord about the outcome of the local elections.

'I wouldn't presume to criticize Your actions,' he wound up, 'but I should never have allowed Peppone to become mayor with a council in which only two people really know how to read and write properly.'

'Culture is entirely without importance, Don Camillo,' replied the Lord with a smile. 'What counts is ideas. Eloquent speeches get nowhere unless there are practical ideas at the back of them. Before judging, suppose we put them to the test.'

'Fair enough,' conceded Don Camillo. 'I really said what I did because, in the event of the lawyers' party coming out top, I had already been given assurances that the bell tower of the church would be repaired. In any case, should it fall down, the people will have compensation in watching the construction of a magnificent People's Palace with dancing, sale of alcoholic liquors, gambling, and a theatre for variety entertainments.'

'And a lock-up for such venomous reptiles as Don Camillo,' added the Lord.

Don Camillo lowered his head. 'Lord, You misjudge me,' he said. 'You know what a cigar means to me? Well, look: this is the only cigar I possess, and look what I am doing with it.'

He pulled a cigar out of his pocket and crumbled it in his enormous hand.

'Well done,' said the Lord. 'Well done, Don Camillo. I accept your penance. Nevertheless, I should like to see you throw away the crumbs, because you would be quite capable of putting them in your pocket and smoking them later on in your pipe.'

'But we are in church,' protested Don Camillo.

'Never mind that, Don Camillo. Throw the tobacco into that corner.' Don Camillo obeyed while the Lord looked on with approval, and just then a knocking was heard at the little door of the sacristy and Peppone came in.

'Good evening, Mr Mayor,' said Don Camillo deferentially.

'Listen,' said Peppone. 'If a Christian is in doubt about something that he has done and comes to tell you about it, and if you found that he had made some mistakes, would you point them out to him or would you simply leave him in ignorance?'

Don Camillo protested indignantly: 'How can you dare to doubt the honesty of a priest? His primary duty is to point out clearly all the penitent's mistakes.'

'Very well, then,' exclaimed Peppone. 'Are you quite ready to hear my confession?'

'I am ready.'

Peppone pulled a large sheet of paper from his pocket and began to read: 'Citizens, at the moment when we are hailing the victorious affirmation of our Party ...'

Don Camillo interrupted him with a gesture and went to kneel before the altar. 'Lord,' he murmured, 'I am no longer responsible for my actions.'

'But I am,' said the Lord promptly. 'Peppone has outwitted you, and you must play fair and do your duty.'

'But, Lord,' persisted Don Camillo. 'You realize, don't You, that You are making me work on behalf of the Agit-Prop?'

'You are working on behalf of grammar, syntax, and spelling, none of which is either diabolical or sectarian.'

Don Camillo put on his spectacles, grasped a pencil, and set to work on the tottering periods of the speech that Peppone was to make on the following day. Peppone read it through intently.

'Good,' he approved. 'There is only one thing that I do not understand. Where I had said: *"It is our intention to extend the schools and to rebuild the bridge over the Fossalto,"* you have substituted: *"It is our intention to extend the schools, repair the church tower, and rebuild the bridge over the Fossalto."* Why is that?'

'A mere matter of syntax,' explained Don Camillo gravely.

'Blessed are those who have studied Latin and who are able to understand niceties of language,' sighed

Peppone. 'And so,' he added, 'we are to lose even the hope that the tower may collapse on to your head!'

Don Camillo raised his arms. 'We must all bow before the will of God!'

When he returned from accompanying Peppone to the door, Don Camillo came to say good night to the Lord.

'Well done, Don Camillo,' said the Lord with a smile. 'I was unjust to you and I am sorry you destroyed your last cigar. It was a penance that you did not deserve. Nevertheless, we may as well be frank about it: Peppone was a skunk not to offer you even a cigar, after all the trouble you took!'

'Oh, all right,' sighed Don Camillo, fishing a cigar from his pocket and preparing to crush it in his big hand.

'No, Don Camillo,' smiled the Lord. 'Go and smoke it in peace. You have earned it.'

'But ...'

'No, Don Camillo; you didn't steal it. Peppone had two cigars in his pocket. Peppone is a Communist. He believes in sharing things. In skilfully relieving him of one cigar, you only took your fair share.'

'You always know best,' exclaimed Don Camillo with deep respect.

6 · THE TREASURE

ONE day Smilzo made his appearance at the presbytery. He was a young ex-partisan who had been Peppone's orderly during the fighting in the mountains and the latter had now taken him on as messenger to the Commune. He was the bearer of a handsome letter printed in Gothic lettering on hand-made paper and with the Party heading.

Your honour is invited to grace with his presence a ceremony of a social nature which will take place tomorrow at ten o'clock a.m. in Piazza della Libertà. The Secretary of the Section, Comrade Bottazzi, Mayor, Giuseppe.

Don Camillo looked severely at Smilzo. 'Tell Comrade Peppone Mayor Giuseppe that I have no wish to go and listen to the usual imbecilities against reaction and the capitalists. I already know them by heart.'

'No,' explained Smilzo. 'This is no affair of political speeches. This is a question of patriotism and social activities. If you refuse it means that you know nothing of democracy.'

Don Camillo nodded his head slowly. 'If that is so,' he said, 'then I have nothing more to say.'

'Very good. And the leader says you are to come in uniform and to bring all your paraphernalia.'

'Paraphernalia?'

'Yes: the pail and the brush; there is something to be blessed.'

Smilzo permitted himself to speak in such a manner to Don Camillo precisely because he was Smilzo – that is to say, the lean one, and so built that by virtue of his amazing swiftness of movement he had been able in the mountains to slip between bullet and bullet without coming to harm. By the time, therefore, that the heavy book flung at him by Don Camillo reached the spot where his head had been, Smilzo had already left the presbytery and was pedalling away for dear life.

Don Camillo got up, rescued the book, and went to let off steam to the Lord at the altar.

'Lord,' he said, 'is it conceivable that I should be unable to find out what those people are planning to do tomorrow? I never knew anything so mysterious. What is the meaning of all these preparations? All those branches that they are sticking into the ground round the meadow between the pharmacy and the Baghettis' house? What kind of devilry can they be up to?'

'My son, if it were devilry, first of all they wouldn't be doing it in the open and secondly they wouldn't be sending for you to bless it. Be patient until tomorrow.'

That evening Don Camillo went to have a look

round but he saw nothing but branches and decorations surrounding the meadow and nobody appeared to know anything.

When he set out next morning, followed by two acolytes, his knees were trembling. He felt that something was not as it should be, that there was treachery in the air.

He returned an hour later, shattered and with a temperature.

'What has happened?' inquired the Lord from the altar.

'Enough to make one's hair stand on end,' stammered Don Camillo. 'A terrible thing. A band, Garibaldi's hymn, a speech from Peppone, and the laying of the foundation stone of the People's Palace! And I had to bless the stone while Peppone chuckled with joy. And the ruffian asked me to say a few words, and I had to make a suitable little address because, although it is a Party activity, the rascal dressed it up as a social undertaking.'

Don Camillo paced to and fro in the empty church. Then he came to a standstill in front of the Lord. 'A mere trifle,' he exclaimed. 'An assembly hall, reading-room, library, gymnasium, dispensary, and theatre. A skyscraper of two floors with adjacent ground for sports and *bocce*. And the whole lot for the miserable sum of ten million lire.'

'By no means dear, given the present prices,' observed the Lord.

Don Camillo sank down upon a bench. 'Lord,' he sighed dolefully, 'why have You done this to me?'

'Don Camillo, you are unreasonable.'

'No: I am not unreasonable. For ten years I have been praying to You on my knees to find me a little money so that I could establish a library, an assembly hall for the young people, a playground for the children with a merry-go-round and swings and possibly a little swimming-pool like they had at Castellino. For ten years I have lowered myself making up to swine of bloated landowners when I should have liked to box their ears every time I saw them. I must have got up quite two hundred lotteries and knocked at quite two thousand doors, and I have nothing at all to show for it. Then along comes this excommunicate mountebank, and behold ten million lire drop into his pockets from heaven.'

The Lord shook His head. 'They didn't fall from heaven,' He replied. 'He found them underground. I had nothing to do with it, Don Camillo. It is entirely due to his own personal initiative.'

Don Camillo spread out his arms. 'Then it is simple enough and the obvious deduction is that I am a poor fool.'

Don Camillo went off to stamp up and down his study in the presbytery, roaring with fury. He must exclude the possibility that Peppone had got himself that ten million by holding people up on the roads or by robbing a bank. 'That fellow, in the days of the liberation, when he came down from the mountains and it seemed as if the proletarian revolution might break out at any moment, must have played upon the funk of those cowards of gentry and squeezed their money out of them.'

Then he reflected that at that time there had been no gentry in the neighbourhood, but that, on the other hand, there had been a detachment of the British Army which had arrived simultaneously with Peppone and his men. The British had taken possession of the gentry's houses, taking the place of the Germans, who, having spent some time in the countryside, had thoroughly cleared those houses of everything of any value. It was therefore out of the question that Peppone should have obtained his ten million by looting.

Possibly the money had come from Russia? He burst

out laughing: was it likely that the Russians should give a thought to Peppone?

At last he returned to the church. 'Lord,' he begged from the foot of the altar, 'won't You tell me where Peppone found the money?'

'Don Camillo,' replied the Lord with a smile, 'do you take Me for a private detective? Why ask God to tell you the truth when you have only to seek it within yourself? Look for it, Don Camillo, and meanwhile, in order to distract your mind, why not make a trip to the town?'

On the following evening, having returned from his excursion to the town, Don Camillo presented himself before the Lord in a condition of extreme agitation.

'What has upset you, Don Camillo?'

'Something quite crazy,' exclaimed Don Camillo breathlessly. 'I have met a dead man! Face to face in the street!'

'Don Camillo, calm yourself and reflect: usually the dead whom one meets face to face in the street are alive.'

'This one cannot be!' shouted Don Camillo. 'This one is dead as mutton, and I know it because I myself carried him to the cemetery.'

'If that is the case,' replied the Lord, 'then I have nothing more to say. You must have seen a ghost.'

Don Camillo shrugged his shoulders. 'Of course not! Ghosts have no existence except in the foolish pates of hysterical women!'

'And therefore?'

'Well ...' muttered Don Camillo.

Don Camillo collected his thoughts. The deceased had been a thin young man, not a native of the village, who had come down from the mountains with Peppone and his men. He had been wounded in the head and was in a bad state, and they had fixed him up in the former German headquarters, which had become the headquarters of the British Command. Peppone had established his own office in the room next to that of the invalid. Don Camillo remembered it all clearly: the villa was surrounded by sentries three deep and not a fly could leave it unperceived, because the British were still fighting nearby and were particularly careful of their own skins.

All this had happened one morning, and on the same evening the young man had died. Peppone had sent for Don Camillo towards midnight, but by the time he had got there the young man had been already in his coffin. The British didn't want the body in the house, and so, at about noon, the coffin, covered with the Italian flag, was carried out of the villa by Peppone and his most trusted men. A detachment of British soldiers had kindly volunteered to supply military honours.

Don Camillo recalled that the ceremony had been moving: all the village had walked behind the coffin, which had been placed on a gun carriage. He himself had made the address before the body was lowered into the grave, and people had actually wept. Peppone, in the front row, had sobbed.

'When I put my mind to it, I certainly know how to express myself!' said Don Camillo to himself complacently, recalling the episode. Then he returned to his original train of thought. 'And in spite of all that, I am prepared to take my oath that the young man whom I met today in the town was the same as the one I followed to the grave.' He sighed. 'Such is life!'

The following day Don Camillo sought out Peppone at his workshop, where he found him lying on his back underneath a car.

'Good morning, Comrade Mayor. I have come to tell you that for the past two days I have been thinking over your description of your People's Palace!'

'And what do you think of it?' jeered Peppone.

'Magnificent! It has made me decide to start work on that scheme of a little place with a bathing-pool, garden, sports ground, theatre, etcetera, which, as you know, I have had in mind for twenty years past. I shall be laying the foundation stone next Sunday. It would give me great pleasure if you, as mayor, would attend the ceremony.'

'Willingly: courtesy for courtesy.'

'In the meanwhile, you might try to cut down the plans for your own place a bit. It looks like being too big for my personal taste.'

Peppone stared at him in amazement. 'Don Camillo, are you demented?'

'Not more than I was when I conducted a funeral and made a patriotic address over a coffin that can't have been securely closed, because only yesterday I met the corpse walking about the town.'

Peppone ground his teeth. 'What are you trying to insinuate?'

'Nothing: only that that coffin to which the British presented arms was full of what you found in the cellars of the Villa Dotti, where the German Command had hidden it. And that the dead man was alive and concealed in the attic.'

'A-a-h!' howled Peppone. 'The same old story! An attempt to malign the partisan movement!'

'Leave the partisans out of it. I take no interest in them!'

And he walked away while Peppone stood muttering vague threats.

That same evening, Don Camillo was awaiting him at the presbytery when he arrived accompanied by Brusco and two other prominent supporters – the same men who had acted as coffin-bearers.

'You,' said Peppone, 'can drop your insinuations. It was all of it stuff looted by the Germans – silver, cameras, instruments, gold, etcetera. If we hadn't taken it, the British would have had it. Ours was the only possible means of getting it out of the place. I have here witnesses and receipts: nobody has touched so much as a lira. Ten million was taken and ten million will be spent for the people.'

Brusco, who was hot-tempered, began to shout that it was God's truth and that he, if necessary, knew well enough how to deal with certain people.

'So do I,' Don Camillo replied calmly. He dropped the newspaper which he had been holding extended in front of himself and thus allowed it to be seen that under his right arm-pit he held the famous tommy-gun that had once belonged to Peppone.

Brusco turned pale and retreated hastily, but Peppone extended his arms. 'Don Camillo, it doesn't seem to me that there is any need to quarrel.'

'I agree,' replied Don Camillo. 'The more easily as I am entirely of your opinion. Ten million was acquired and ten million should be spent on the people. Seven on your People's Palace and three on my recreation centre for the people's children. Suffer the little children to come unto me. I ask only what is my due.'

The four consulted together for a moment in undertones. Then Peppone spoke: 'If you hadn't got that damnable thing in your hands, I should tell you that your suggestion is the filthiest blackmail in the universe.'

On the following Sunday Peppone, together with all the village council, assisted in the laying of the foundation stone of Don Camillo's recreation centre. He also made a short speech. However, he found a means of whispering in Don Camillo's ear:

'It might be better to tie this stone round your neck and throw you into the Po.'

That evening Don Camillo went to make his report to the Lord above the altar.

'Well; what do You think about it?' he said in conclusion.

'Exactly what Peppone said to you. That if you hadn't got that damnable thing in your hands, I should say that it was the filthiest blackmail in the universe.'

'But I have nothing at all in my hands except the cheque that Peppone has just given me.'

'Precisely,' whispered the Lord. 'And with that three million you are going to do so many beautiful things, Don Camillo, that I haven't the heart to scold you.'

Don Camillo genuflected and went off to bed to dream of a garden full of children – a garden with a merry-go-round and a swing, and seated on the swing Peppone's youngest son chirping joyfully like a fledgling.

7 · NOCTURNE WITH BELLS

FOR some time Don Camillo had felt that he was being watched. On turning round suddenly when he was walking along the street or in the fields he saw no one, but felt convinced that if he had looked behind a hedge or among the bushes he would have found a pair of eyes and all that goes with them.

When leaving the presbytery on a couple of evenings he not only heard a sound from behind the door, but he caught a glimpse of a shadow.

'Let it be,' the Lord had replied from above the altar when Don Camillo had asked Him for advice. 'Eyes never did anyone any harm.'

'But it would be useful to know whether those two eyes are going about alone or accompanied by a third, for instance one of 9-calibre,' sighed Don Camillo. 'That is a detail not without its own importance.'

'Nothing can defeat a good conscience, Don Camillo.'

'I know, Lord,' sighed Don Camillo once more, 'but the trouble is that people don't usually fire at a conscience, but between the shoulders.'

However, Don Camillo did nothing about the matter and a little time elapsed, and then late one evening when he was sitting alone in the presbytery reading, he unexpectedly 'felt' the eyes upon him.

There were three of them, and raising his head slowly he saw first of all the black eye of a revolver and then those of Biondo.

'Do I lift my hands?' inquired Don Camillo quietly.

'I don't want to do you any harm,' replied Biondo, thrusting the revolver into his jacket pocket. 'I was afraid you might be scared when I appeared unexpectedly and might start shouting.'

'I understand,' replied Don Camillo. 'And did it never strike you that by simply knocking at the door you could have avoided all this trouble?'

Biondo made no reply; he went and leaned over the windowsill. Then he turned round suddenly and sat down beside Don Camillo's little table. His hair was ruffled, his eyes deeply circled, and his forehead was damp with sweat.

'Don Camillo,' he muttered from behind clenched teeth, 'that fellow at the house near the dyke; it was I that did him in.'

Don Camillo lighted a cigar. 'The house near the dyke?' he said quietly. 'Well, that's an old story; it was a political affair and came within the terms of amnesty. What are you worrying about? You're all right under the law.'

Biondo shrugged his shoulders. 'To hell with the

amnesty,' he said furiously. 'Every night when I put my light out I can feel him near my bed, and I can't understand what it means.'

Don Camillo puffed a cloud of blue smoke into the air. 'Nothing at all, Biondo,' he replied with a smile. 'Listen to me: go to sleep with the light on.'

Biondo sprang to his feet. 'You can go and jeer at that fool Peppone,' he shouted, 'but you can't do it to me!'

Don Camillo shook his head. 'Firstly, Peppone is not a fool; and, secondly, where you are concerned there is nothing that I can do for you.'

'If I must buy candles or make an offering to the church, I'll pay,' shouted Biondo, 'but you've got to absolve me. And in any case I'm all right legally!'

'I agree, my son,' said Don Camillo mildly. 'But the trouble is that no one has ever yet made an amnesty for consciences. Therefore, so far as we are concerned, we muddle along in the same old way, and in order to obtain absolution it is necessary to be penitent and then to act in a manner that is deserving of forgiveness. It's a lengthy affair.'

Biondo sniggered. 'Penitent? Penitent of having done in that fellow? I'm only sorry I didn't bag the lot!'

'That is a province in which I am completely incompetent. On the other hand, if your conscience tells you that you acted rightly, then you should be content,' said Don Camillo, opening a book and laying it in front of Biondo. 'Look, we have very clear rules that do not exclude the political field. Fifth: thou shalt not kill. Seventh: thou shalt not steal.'

'What has that got to do with it?' inquired Biondo in a mystified voice.

'Nothing,' Don Camillo reassured him, 'but I had an idea that you told me that you had killed him, under the cloak of politics, in order to steal his money.'

'I never said so!' shouted Biondo, pulling out his

pistol and thrusting it into Don Camillo's face. 'I never said so, but it's true! And if it's true and you dare to tell a living soul I shall blow you to pieces!'

'We don't tell such things even to the Eternal Father,' Don Camillo reassured him; 'and in any case He knows them better than we do.'

Biondo appeared to quiet down. He opened his hand and looked at his weapon. 'Now look at that!' he exclaimed, laughing. 'I hadn't even noticed that the safety catch was down.'

He raised the catch with a careful finger.

'Don Camillo,' said Biondo in a strange voice. 'I am sick of seeing that fellow standing near my bed. There are only two ways for it: either you absolve me or I shoot you.' The pistol shook slightly in his hand and Don Camillo turned rather pale and looked him straight in the eyes.

'Lord,' said Don Camillo mentally, 'this is a mad dog and he will fire. An absolution given in such conditions is valueless. What do I do?'

'If you are afraid, give him absolution,' replied the voice of the Lord.

Don Camillo folded his arms on his breast.

'No, Biondo,' said Don Camillo.

Biondo set his teeth. 'Don Camillo, give me absolution or I fire.'

'No.'

Biondo pulled the trigger and the trigger yielded, but there was no explosion.

And then Don Camillo struck, and his blow did not miss the mark, because Don Camillo's punches never misfired.

Then he flung himself up the steps of the tower and rang the bells furiously for twenty minutes. And all the countryside declared that Don Camillo had gone mad, with the exception of the Lord above the altar, who shook His head, smiling, and Biondo, who, tearing across the fields like a lunatic, had reached the bank of the river and was about to throw himself into its dark waters. Then he heard the bells.

So Biondo turned back because he had heard a Voice that he had never known. And that was the real miracle, because a pistol that misfires is a material event, but a priest who begins to ring joybells at eleven o'clock at night is quite another matter.

8 · VICTIMS OF WAR

MILCO didn't know how to begin, but finally he managed to say:

'It's about that German woman. Today is the twenty-sixth, and she'll be here the day after tomorrow.'

He seemed to be intensely worried, and Don Camillo couldn't see why.

'Every twenty-eighth of March since 1946 she's descended upon you. She may just as well come this year, too.'

Milco shook his head.

'You don't know the whole story, Father,' muttered Milco; 'that's why you can't understand.'

True enough, Don Camillo knew no more than did the rest of the village. The story went back to the end of September 1943, when a small detachment of Germans had occupied the village. Among them was Sergeant Fritz, who functioned as quartermaster. He himself was lodged in Milco's house at La Torretta, not very far from the village, between the highway and the Stivone River.

At this time Milco was thirty years old, but he had stayed at home because of a lame leg and also because, in spite of this disability, he was the only man able to run the farm. Milco's wife was not strong, and his extremely healthy son was only eleven years old. There were no other members of the family, and in time of war, when agriculture is just as important as heavy industry, there can be no question of leaving the land deserted and unproductive.

Sergeant Fritz was a good-natured fellow, the same age as Milco, who went about making war as another man might have gone about store-keeping or accounting. Good German that he was, he had a weakness for Italian wine, and when he had drunk a bit more than necessary he would pull out of his wallet the photograph of a handsome, blond young woman and a ten-month-old blond baby boy, which invariably moved him to tears.

Sergeant Fritz was happy in Milco's house, and both Milco and his wife treated him like one of the family. He had a happy-go-lucky temperament, and since he was in charge of the commissary department he never came back to the farm empty-handed. The sergeant stayed in Milco's house until 28 March 1945. On the evening of that day he did not come back, and the next day he was fished out of the Stivone River, near Brugello. But it was plain that he had not drowned, for three bullets from a P-38 had gone clean through his head. In those days the Partisans were very active, and Sergeant Fritz had run into one of their bands.

The twenty-eighth of March after the war was over, a blond young German woman and her blond baby came to La Torretta. The woman knew about four words of Italian and Milco knew about four words of German, so that they were able to understand one another.

'I am the widow of Sergeant Fritz,' she told him, 'and I have come to lay flowers on his tomb.'

Milco took her to the cemetery, and she laid her flowers at the foot of the crude wooden cross on which was written the Sergeant's life story:

Fritz Hauser
2 March 1915–28 March 1945

Milco and his wife asked the woman and her child to stay with them for a whole week. The woman talked about the dreadful conditions in Germany and the difficulties she had encountered on her trip. But above all she talked about Fritz. She said that Fritz had written her a very moving account of Milco and his family, and that she had come not only to visit his tomb but also to pay a tribute of gratitude to them, in short, to thank them for all they had done for her husband.

'I had to sell every last bit of gold I possessed in order to make the journey,' she told them. 'Now I have nothing. But I hope to find a job, so that next year I shall have another money to come see you again.'

She kept her word, and turned up promptly the next year and the one that followed. Punctually, on every twenty-eighth of March, she came with her child to stay for a week at La Torretta. By now everyone in the village knew her and her story. Whenever they met her in the street, they greeted her profusely because, among other things, she was 'a fine figure of a girl'. She had the generously proportioned sort of beauty which is especially appreciated in the fertile Po valley.

Don Camillo was still perplexed.

'I don't see what it is that requires such special understanding,' he muttered. 'No one can criticize you for letting her stay in your house, even if you're a widower. After all, you don't live there alone; you have your son and his policewoman of a wife with you. And your wife – God rest her soul! – was already dead when this German woman came last year. What has happened since then to change the situation?'

Milco hesitated for a moment and then said abruptly: 'I simply don't want to see her again!'

Don Camillo shrugged his shoulders.

'Well, then, why have you come to me? That's none of my business. If you don't like her face, just write her a letter and tell her to stay away.'

But Milco had something more on his mind, as was plain to see from the way he twisted his hat in his hands.

'As long as my wife was alive, I could talk things out with her. But now, who is there for me to talk to?'

By now the channel of communication was opened, and Don Camillo had only to let Milco have his say.

'Father, you remember how it was. I was tied up with the Resistance movement, and they had put me in charge of transmitting their radio messages. I had the radio hidden under a barrel in my barn. On the evening of 28 March 1945 Fritz caught me red-handed ...'

'Fritz caught you?' stammered Don Camillo.

'Yes. As usual, after we'd finished supper, I said: "I'm going to have a game of cards with Ronchini." And as usual, he said: "Good luck to you!" I went out and started to walk across the fields, but when I reached the beech-tree I stayed there for a quarter of an hour and then retraced my steps. There was a little door at the rear of the barn which I was the only one ever to use. I slipped through it and took out the transmitting apparatus, just as I had done a hundred times before. But this time the worst possible thing happened: Fritz burst in and caught me at it ...'

He paused and wiped the perspiration off his forehead.

'A light went on, and there was Fritz standing before me, quite beside himself with rage. "Traitor!" he shouted, with his hand on the butt of his pistol. I had my own finger on the trigger of a loaded P-38, which was always in my pocket, and I beat him to the draw ... Cursed war! ...'

And he stopped again to wipe his forehead.

'If he hadn't called me "Traitor", perhaps I wouldn't have shot him, but the word sounded like a death sentence ... It was dark and rainy outside. I loaded his body on my shoulders, carried it down to the river, and threw it in. The Stivone was running high and the body was swept a couple of miles downstream, to the place where it was later found. No one had the slightest suspicion. My wife was the only one ever to know, and now she's dead.'

Don Camillo pondered for several minutes over this story. Finally he muttered:

'What can I say? Am I to call you a patriot or an assassin? Your own conscience must be your guide.'

'That's why I'm here,' Milco exclaimed. 'I can't look at it from the patriotic angle. Even if I were to get a medal, I'd still consider myself guilty of murdering Fritz. I can't sleep at night ... The first time that German woman came and started to thank me for all I'd done for her dead husband, I thought I'd go through the floor with shame ... I killed him and she thanks me! And the fatherless child calls me uncle! No, I can't stand it any longer. I can't live through fifty-one weeks of the year dreading the fifty-second. I don't want ever to see her again; I don't want my stomach to turn over. Father, you can't imagine what I've gone through in the last ten years.'

'Yes, I can imagine,' said Don Camillo. 'And I'm glad that you suffered. It shows that your conscience is working.'

'Yes, it is,' said Milco excitedly. 'That's why I came here. I'm not looking for comfort. You can say what you please, but the fact remains that I murdered Fritz. You'll have to help me shake off that woman. I haven't the heart to do it, but surely you can tell her the whole story.'

'I?' exclaimed Don Camillo, with wide-open eyes.

'Yes. She's arriving the day after tomorrow. You must talk to her . . . It isn't right that she should thank me for my kindness and treat me like a friend. I'm taking something that isn't due. She must be told that I killed her husband, and then she must tell her son. That way she'll never come back, and my sufferings will be at an end.'

Don Camillo shook his head.

'No, Milco, if you really have a conscience, then you mustn't seek to evade further suffering. It's not enough to repent; you must make amends as well. If the sight of this woman makes you suffer, then you must thank God for letting you see her. And why should you wish to hurt her still more? Aren't you satisfied with having killed her husband?'

Milco waved his arms wildly.

'Of course I don't want to hurt her!'

'Well, that's just what you're going to do. She trusts you and thinks of you as one of the family, and you'd rob her of this last illusion. If her presence gives you pain, so much the better. I'll say a prayer for you.'

After Milco had gone away, Don Camillo went

into the church to pray for him. But it was a very strange prayer.

'Lord,' Don Camillo said to the Christ on the altar, 'in this filthy land, there are tens of thousands of persons who killed tens of thousands of others. And they're not sorry; in fact they brag about it. They want medals and positions; they want to be deputies to parliament, senators, and publishers; they want their pictures in the school-books of the nation! ... Now here's a poor devil who has suffered ten years just because he killed a man, and we are powerless to help him. We can't say: "Look here, Milco ... When Fritz caught you with the radio, he called you a traitor, didn't he? Well, you could have called him the same thing! While you were in the barn working for the Resistance Movement, your wife, abetted by Sergeant Fritz, was working for Germany ... without thought of resistance!" ... No, Lord, we can't tell this to Milco, because his wife revealed it on her death-bed, and a priest can't violate the secret of the confessional. Lord, You know best, but is it right, I ask you?'

'Yes, it is, Don Camillo,' Christ answered. 'The sin of the wife doesn't cancel the sin of the husband. Each one has to pay ...'

March 28 rolled round, and with it came the Germans. As soon as Don Camillo heard of their arrival he hurried out to La Torretta, where Milco greeted him like a long-lost friend. It was a fine, sunny day and while the little boy played in the yard with the dog, his mother, Milco, and Don Camillo went to look at the fields, which were just stirring from their long hibernation.

'You haven't much colour in your cheeks,' said Don Camillo to the German woman.

'I work at a factory in a big city, where there's lots of smoke,' she explained.

'That's no good,' said Don Camillo gravely. 'And don't you have to pinch and scrape all year in order to make this visit?'

'I don't mind pinching and scraping,' she answered with a smile.

'Why don't you come and live here, near Fritz?' said Don Camillo. 'That would make Fritz happy, I'm sure.'

She stared at him in amazement.

'Don't you like it here?' Don Camillo asked her.

'Oh, very much! Italy is the most wonderful place! But I have a home and a job ...'

Don Camillo waved in the direction of Milco's house.

'Why not have a home and a job here?'

Don Camillo had no gift for parlour games, and so he came straight to the point:

'You marry him ... he marries you ... I perform the ceremony ... that way everyone will be happy!'

The woman was thirty-seven years old, but she still knew how to blush and proceeded to do so. Milco was forty-two and too old for blushing, but he turned pale. Don Camillo was no matchmaker, and now embarrassment overcame him.

'Very well,' he said. 'Think it over. When you're ready you'll find me in my office. *Guten Abend.*'

And with that he went away.

Apparently they did think it over, for three days later Milco came to see him.

'Well, Father, you shall have your way, and we'll get married.'

'Exactly. It's your way, too, I trust.'

Milco heaved a sigh.

'Here's hoping that to have her around all the time won't give me more pain than ever. If my conscience still hurts me ...'

'Let's get this straight, Milco,' said Don Camillo. 'Where Fritz is concerned, things are just the same. You took away his life, and you can't restore it. That will have to stay on your conscience. But when it comes to the woman and child, it's a different matter. You deprived her of her husband, but you're giving her another ... and there'll no longer be a fatherless boy. Don't mix your accounts!'

'God help me, that's all I can say!' exclaimed Milco.

'He's helped you already!' retorted Don Camillo.

9 · A SPEECH TO GO DOWN IN HISTORY

'For that meeting on the twenty-sixth, we've got to think up something special,' Peppone said gravely.

Bigio, Brusco, and Smilzo all looked puzzled, and Peppone hastened to enlighten them.

'We're lucky enough to have our rally scheduled as the last one before the election, which means that no matter what we say no one can contradict it. But we're called upon for some substantial oratory, not just the usual hot air. There's no question of bringing in a speaker from outside, because this is a local election, and we're on our own. We've got to produce something smashing, something that will go down in history.'

His three aides relaxed. If this was all he had on his mind, there was no need to worry.

'Chief, we're riding the crest of the wave,' Smilzo answered gaily. 'All you have to do is drive the last nail in their coffin!'

Peppone shook his head.

'A concluding speech is no joke. Election eve is not the time for a political harangue. It's got to be something factual: a record of past accomplishments and a pledge of others to come. It's one thing to promise social justice, and another to date the opening of a public laundry. Big ideas are all very well for a national election, but on the local level it's better to stick to the concrete. The question is how to make parish-pump politics sound epoch-making.'

Smilzo continued to dissent.

'If a fellow knows what he wants to say, it's simple enough to say it.'

'Simple, indeed!' retorted Peppone. 'But one point I grant you. It's a question not of just the appropriate thing, but of what you *want* to say. An historical speech can't be improvised; it must be thought out in advance, with every word weighed and every effect calculated. Words aren't enough; you've got to know their meanings. It takes spadework with the dictionary.'

'You have a big enough vocabulary, Chief,' Smilzo assured him. 'Why work so hard over it?'

'A big vocabulary isn't enough, I tell you,' shouted Peppone. 'I need peace and quiet, for purposes of meditation. That's why I've called you together. Even if the People's Palace goes up in smoke, or Togliatti himself makes a tour of inspection, yes, even come the revolution, I'm not to be disturbed. No one must break the continuity of my speech. Have I made myself clear?'

They understood him perfectly.

'Chief,' said Smilzo, 'even if we have to guard your

house with machine-guns, no one shall come near you. Just leave it to us!'

This is why, at a certain point, Peppone disappeared from circulation.

Just as election day was drawing close and the atmosphere was growing hotter and hotter, when his enemies were showing their claws and a strong hand was needed to put them in their place, Peppone vanished from sight. Had he been taken ill? Purged? Gone underground? Sent on a secret mission? His workshop was silent and the sign hanging on the door carried the simple word 'Closed'. The windows and doors of his own house were barred and his children were staying at their grandmother's, with not a word to be got out of them. Even his wife was gone.

Don Camillo sent out spies and alerted all the gossipy old women of the village. He himself walked by Peppone's house, but found no clue to the mystery. But in a village so small that everyone knew everything about his neighbour, such a situation could not long endure. News leaked through to the rectory that Peppone's house was not deserted, that his wife had been seen at the window and every night Smilzo delivered a parcel there and then came home empty-handed. Smilzo was tailed and found to be going every day to buy food at Castelletto, food sufficient to fill two hungry mouths. When it was discovered that Smilzo also bought cigars, then it was obvious that although one of the mouths might belong to Peppone's wife, the other indubitably belonged to Peppone. Decoys dogged Smilzo's footsteps, and one evening he let them treat him to too many glasses of sparkling red Lambrusco wine. They brought up the subject of politics and remarked how strange it was that Peppone should be absent from the scene. One of the decoys said argumentatively:

'There's nothing so strange about it. It's a bad case

of yellow liver. He knows the game is up and doesn't dare show his face.'

'Just wait till you hear his historical speech, after all the work he's putting into it!' said Smilzo, falling like a ton of bricks for their little game.

Five minutes later Don Camillo was informed, but the news did not disturb him.

'Is that all?' he puffed. 'Not worth talking about!'

And indeed he did not bring up the subject again. But that very night an unknown hand wrote on Peppone's door:

> Here lies Comrade Giuseppe Bottazzi,
> Who has sought solitude
> In order to write an historical election-eve oration.
> The question is whether, when it's written,
> He'll know how to read it.

Although Don Camillo had dismissed the matter as unworthy of mention, this epigraph caused all malicious tongues to wag about it. Such tongues are not too numerous in the Po valley, or at least there is no more than one to every inhabitant, and not the six or seven which seem to be the sources of so vast a volume of gossip.

Meanwhile the blissfully ignorant Peppone continued to toil over his epoch-making speech. His faithful and discreet wife moved about the house in bedroom slippers in order not to break its continuity. Peppone had never worked so hard in all his life. He worked as hard as if he were forging a hundred-foot iron fence, complete with an ornate gate. The stakes were high. His enemies were dead set on getting into power, whereas Peppone and his gang sought their third consecutive re-election. What with weighing every word and polishing every sentence, Peppone expended far more time than he had imagined, and the final touches were added no earlier than the Friday morning before the historical

Saturday night. Then, oddly enough, the scribbler's prophecy was fulfilled, and Peppone was unable to read what he had written. Fortunately, this possibility had been taken into consideration. Smilzo had been standing by for two days, and now he took over the precious manuscript, jumped on to his motor-cycle, and rode madly to the city, where a loyal typist proceeded to tap out two copies, one for Peppone and the other for ... history.

It was late at night and Don Camillo was about to go to bed when Caroline, a poor old creature that went about collecting wood and stale bread, brought him a cardboard folder.

'I found it on the edge of a ditch down near *La Pioppaccia*,' she told him. 'It's full of papers and they may be important to someone. Can you say something about it in church and see if there are any claimants?'

After she had gone away Don Camillo examined the papers. Soon he realized, to his amazement, that he had Peppone's historical speech in hand, the original and two copies.

Meanwhile Smilzo was sitting under a poplar on the river bank, with death in his heart. He had lost the folder containing the speech. It had slipped out of his pocket while he was riding home, full speed, from the city. Twice he had retraced a portion of the route, vainly searching, and then he had sat down to nurse his despair.

'If I come back empty-handed, the chief will kill me,' he said to himself over and over.

And he was not far from right.

Peppone spent an agonizing night. After waiting and waiting for Smilzo to come, he put in a long-distance telephone call. The typist told him that Smilzo had left four hours before, with the masterpiece under his arm. Then he called his general staff, and they sent out search-parties. At four o'clock in the morning, there was still no news of Smilzo, and Peppone, who had been angrily pacing up and down the hall, suddenly collapsed.

'Traitor!' he exclaimed, and let himself be carried off to bed, where he fell into a leaden sleep, accompanied by a high fever.

Smilzo turned up at Bigio's house at nine o'clock. When Bigio heard that the speech was lost he was speechless with dismay. He stared hard at Smilzo and said:

'You may as well emigrate to Venezuela.'

New orders were sent out to the search-parties. They were to stop looking for Smilzo and watch out for a yellow folder which the miserable fellow had lost on the road. A large-scale manoeuvre of this kind could not escape attention. People took note, asked questions, gossiped, put two and two together, and came, by afternoon, to this conclusion: the text of Peppone's famous speech was lost and that evening he would find himself in exceedingly hot water. Which meant that a large crowd would gather to see him squirm.

The meeting was to start at nine o'clock, and by half past eight the square was full. At this last minute Peppone's henchmen collected their courage and went to wake him. They had quite a job to get him even to open his eyes. He was still feverish and his eyelids were leaden. They explained that a huge crowd had gathered in the square and he must make up his mind what to do.

'How about Smilzo?' Peppone asked in a dim faraway voice.

'He's found,' said Bigio.

'And the speech?' Peppone panted.

'It's lost,' said Bigio, prudently retreating three steps.

But he need not have been so cautious. Peppone was too far gone to be a menace. He simply closed his eyes and sighed.

'Chief, what are we going to do?' asked Bigio anxiously.

'Go to the devil, the lot of you,' murmured Peppone, as if in a dream.

'What about the crowd? And the Party?'

'Devil take the crowd and the Party too,' said Peppone pacifically.

His henchmen stared at one another. This was the end.

'There's nothing we can do,' said Bigio. 'We'll have to tell the crowd that the meeting is adjourned because the speaker is ill.'

Just then Don Camillo appeared upon the scene. Obviously he did not expect to find Peppone so stricken, and he looked down in bewilderment at the inert form on the bed. He did not say a word or make his presence felt in any way, but in a few moments Peppone opened first one eye and then the other.

'I'm not ready yet for Extreme Unction,' he muttered.

'Too bad,' said Don Camillo.

'You can go; I don't need you.'

'You always need me, Comrade!' said Don Camillo, taking a big yellow folder out of his pocket and throwing it on to the bed. Peppone reached out, opened it and stared at the contents.

'Check it, now, Comrade,' said Don Camillo, with a laugh. 'Everything's there: the original manuscript and two copies. Remember that "incontrovertible" takes only one *b* and be thankful to your parish priest.'

Peppone slowly slipped the papers back into the folder and hoisted himself into a sitting position. Then he clenched his teeth, looked into Don Camillo's eyes, and said brusquely:

'I'd rather not thank him.'

Peppone's hands were as big as shovels. With a single gesture he ripped the folder and its contents in two, then, as if he were prey to some uncontrollable madness, he tore both pieces into shreds, rolled them up in a ball and threw them out of the window. Next, he leaped out of bed.

It was nine o'clock, and the crowd in the square was beginning to murmur, when suddenly Peppone walked on to the platform. His fever had fallen, or rather it was not the same sort of fever. This was clear at once from the way he said: 'Fellow-citizens! ...' The crowd was silent and Peppone spoke. He improvised; a dozen times he said 'ain't' and 'don't' for 'isn't' and 'doesn't'; he referred to the 'Nemesis of history' and the 'Nemesis of geography', but the most awkward phrases quite plainly came from a full heart, so that even his severest critics had to admit that he was a good fellow.

So it was that Smilzo didn't emigrate to Venezuela and Peppone was re-elected mayor, without having to thank Don Camillo, but indebted, none the less, to Divine Providence for preventing him from pronouncing a speech that would have gone down in history as abysmally stupid. And Don Camillo was not too perturbed by the outcome of the election, for he knew that in politics we can often obtain more from our enemies than from our friends.

10 · PEPPONE GOES BACK TO SCHOOL

PEPPONE decided to go all out against clerical interference in the primary schools, and an announcement to this effect came out in the bulletin nailed to the wall of the People's Palace. In it was the proposal that a supervisory committee be set up and empowered to visit the schools at any time to make sure that the teaching was in accord with democratic principles.

Of course, the next day, the bulletin of the Opposition printed a reply:

We don't for a moment criticize our Mayor for the fact

that he never finished school. We believe that ideas are much more important than good grammar. But for purposes of the present discussion we must note that it seems singularly inappropriate for primary instruction to be in the hands of someone who never finished his own. Let the Mayor hand over this job to Smilzo, who stayed two years in first grade and three years in both second and third, thus acquiring considerably more experience in the field of education.

This piece caused considerable talk in the village, and Don Camillo made a copy of it which he took to read to the Christ over the altar.

'I am still of the same opinion,' Christ told him. 'This was written by a man just as stupid as the one who pencilled the word "Donkey!" on the margin of some other declaration by Peppone.'

'But, Lord,' Don Camillo objected, 'this is an entirely different matter. Isn't it stupid of a man with one leg to insist on entering a race?'

'Don Camillo, you're not playing fair! A man with only one leg can't acquire another in its place, but a man who doesn't know grammar can always learn it. If you know the person who wrote these words, tell him that they are very stupid.'

'I'll try to explain,' said Don Camillo, throwing out his arms, 'but it's going to be uphill work, because he honestly believes he's in the right.'

'He can't honestly believe that, when he's out of harmony with God's law. You know that perfectly well, because I've told you.'

'Don Camillo is always in hot water,' the priest sighed.

Peppone couldn't take the counter-attack lying down, and so he brought out another broadside:

We can confidantly state that if our unknown adversary were to look after his priestly affairs instead of the affairs of other people, it would be a very good thing. There are two kinds of ignorance: the ignorance of those who for obvious reasons have not been able to continue their schooling and that of persons like the ignorant priest in question, who has studied a great deal but learned nothing. He reminds us of a shiny copper pot, with a hole in the bottom, looking down at a tarnished old pot, which is obviously much more serviceable for cooking.

This was only the beginning, and the rest was couched in much grosser terms. When Don Camillo went to kneel in front of the altar, Christ asked him if he had read Peppone's new innuendo.

'Yes, Lord.'

'And have you resisted the temptation to reply?'

'Yes, Lord.'

'Will you be able to keep up your resistance?'

Don Camillo threw out his arms.

'The future is in God's hands,' he answered.

'But the draft of your reply is in your right hand pocket, and so in this case the future is in the hands of Don Camillo.'

Don Camillo took the sheet of paper out of his pocket and burned it in the flame of a candle.

'The election is just around the corner,' he observed, 'and to my mind these are mistaken tactics, from a political point of view.'

'That may be, Don Camillo. But don't worry about the election. I'm not for or against any ticket. I won my battle a long time ago.'

When Peppone was beside himself with political passion, he proceeded with about as much delicacy as a Sherman tank, and so, naturally enough, this piece of prose which began with the famous 'confid*a*ntly' was full of errors. People laughed immoderately at it, even without any instigation on the part of Don Camillo, and Peppone's pride was deeply injured. He tried throwing a few punches around and received a few from persons upon whom he had not inflicted any, but he was aware that this did not alter the situation and that his grammar was just as stumbling as ever. And so he dropped the fight for a supervisory committee and fastened his energies upon the fulfilment of a very ambitious dream. No one except his wife knew anything about it. Every evening, when he set off on his motorcycle, she gave an anxious sigh, and towards midnight, when he returned she immediately asked:

'How did you do?'

'It's hard going, but I'll make it.'

This went on for three and a half months, until one night, upon his return from the mysterious trip, Peppone announced:

'This is it! I'm taking the plunge!'

'What if you don't succeed?'

'I must, that's all.'

'Think how those wretched people will laugh if you fail. Couldn't you do it in the city, where nobody knows you and if you don't make the grade, it doesn't matter?'

'No, if I did it anywhere else, they'd say there was something tricky or dishonest about it. It's got to be done in the light of day, with everything legal. I'm putting in an application tomorrow.'

'Well, be sure not to make any mistakes in the application!'

'You don't need to worry about that,' Peppone reassured her. 'I've got the application all ready. They typed it up for me in the city!'

I, Giuseppe Bottazzi, etc., etc., respectfully ask permission of the Board of Education to take the eighth-grade examinations ...

The bomb burst with a noise almost atomic in intensity, and Smilzo ran to Peppone's house with his eyes popping out of his head.

'Chief, people are saying that you want to take the eighth-grade examinations!'

'Well, what's so remarkable about it?'

'Chief, the eighth grade is tough!'

'Good! "Live dangerously!" must be our motto.'

'Chief, if you fail, you're a goner!'

'Verdi failed at the Conservatory, and then did pretty well.'

In the face of such confidence, Smilzo could find nothing to say. With all the nonchalance of a gentleman flicking an ash off the end of his cigarette, Peppone added:

'If I haven't got an inferiority complex, why should you have one?'

This was the last straw. If Peppone knew the meaning of an inferiority complex, then he must be up to his ears in culture.

'Chief,' Smilzo stammered, 'have you been studying all these months? It must have cost you an awful lot of money?'

'Why? I took a cramming course at a night school in the city, for adults and children together. At the desk next to mine there was a twelve-year-old boy called Mario Bibelli, a little fellow that didn't come up to my shoulder. He'll pay me a visit here some Sunday.'

'Amazing!' exclaimed Smilzo. 'It sounds like an old-fashioned romantic novel.'

'Reality is the true romanticism of both yesterday and today,' said Peppone didactically. 'Both De Amicis and De Sica are neo-realists, even if the former did his writing a century ago.'

Smilzo went away completely convinced of one thing: Peppone had turned into an intellectual.

'It wouldn't surprise me if he were to write for some literary magazine,' he said to Brusco, Bigio, and the rest of Peppone's henchmen. 'This is going to be a bitter pill for some people to swallow.'

It was a bitter pill for Don Camillo, who was burning up with eagerness to talk to Peppone and size up his new education. Peppone seemed to be avoiding him, and this exasperated his curiosity all the further. Finally he did get hold of him, by means of a personal visit to the workshop. Peppone greeted him with gentlemanly indifference.

'What can I do for you?' he asked.

'I was just passing by,' said Don Camillo, 'and wanted to inquire about the health of our mayor.'

'There's no mayor here. Here you have only Giuseppe Bottazzi, the blacksmith, descendant of the blacksmith of the same name who brought the family to this village several centuries ago and was beheaded because he stripped a priest of his ill-gotten gains. There's the nemesis of history for you!'

'The nemesis of history? How do you mean?' asked Don Camillo in utter astonishment.

'I mean that maybe this time there'll be a different ending and Giuseppe Bottazzi will not only strip the priest of his ill-gotten gains, but kill him!'

'Ill-gotten gains? But I have no more money than a jumping jack-rabbit!'

'I'm not speaking of money. You've captured the confidence of a great many ignorant people, and we shall take it away!'

The conversation was taking an unpleasant turn, but Don Camillo swallowed his pride for the sake of acquiring further information.

'What will be, will be,' he said. 'How about the examinations?'

'Trifles!' answered Peppone. 'The important examination is the one I take every day with this hammer and anvil. And I pass it, time after time.'

As Don Camillo was going away, he saw Peppone's wife at the door.

'Did you come to rag him?' she said aggressively. 'It's

eating you up, isn't it, that you can't brand him as someone that never got through school?'

'No,' said Don Camillo. 'But it's still too early to say. We'll see what happens when he's put to the test.'

Don Camillo went home in a gloomy state of mind.

'Lord,' he said to the Christ over the altar, 'that poor fellow is so swollen with pride that he deserves to fail every single subject.'

'I don't know about that, Don Camillo. I'm not on the examination committee. That's for them to decide.'

'God is everywhere,' objected Don Camillo, 'and He'll be in the schoolroom where that country bumpkin comes to make a fool of himself.'

'Certainly, Don Camillo, God is everywhere. Right now He's listening to the stupid things you are saying.'

Don Camillo threw out his arms in discouragement. 'For some time now, I haven't been able to say the right thing!'

The matter of examining Mayor Peppone was a headache to the Board of Education. Things had to be conducted with such scrupulous care that no one could find an excuse for saying that either success or failure was due to the candidate's political office or party affiliation. A special commission was made up of the board's director and two teachers from another township, one a stiff, elderly woman and the other a middle-aged man. Peppone was in a radiant mood, with no doubts at all as to his ability to get through. When he received notice that the examinations would be held the next day he burst out with:

'It's about time! I was beginning to be thoroughly bored.'

He went to bed in a good humour and got up in one that was even better. Immediately he put on his best suit, filled his fountain-pen, tested it on a piece of paper, and started to leave the house.

'I'll go with you as far as the school,' his wife suggested.

'Don't let's be silly about it!' said Peppone.

'Your son insists on going,' she told him.

'Don't make me look ridiculous; I'd seem like a schoolboy, and all those wretched people will be staring out their windows at me.'

And so Peppone went off alone, but when he reached the school, his wife and son were already there, lurking behind a hedge, all red in the face from having run across the fields to beat him. As he started up the steps into the schoolhouse, they waved to him and he waved back at them with his hand hidden halfway down his back. The commission welcomed him with icy politeness.

'Sit down,' said the director. 'You will have written examinations in arithmetic and composition. Remember that the allotted time is four hours.'

Then they set before him four sheets of officially stamped examination paper, two for a rough copy and two for the finished product.

'Shall we begin?' asked the director, after Peppone had sat down and taken out his pen.

'By all means,' said Peppone.

'Then take this down: "Problem: A cement basin of parallelepiped form has a base 40 by 60 centimetres in size is fed by two taps. The first tap pours in 8 litres of water a minute and the second tap 5 litres of water every other minute. In thirty minutes the flow from the second tap alone fills two-fifths of the basin. How long will it take to fill the whole basin if both taps are open? How high is the basin?"'

As Peppone diligently wrote down the problem, he noticed that his hand had begun to tremble. 'I shouldn't have done so much hammering last night,' he said to himself. 'It has tired my hand.' Meanwhile the director told him to shift to another sheet of paper and take down the composition theme set for him by the woman teacher.

'Theme: Narrate some event, either recent or long ago, which made a strong impression upon you.'

Peppone took this down with some difficulty, for his hand continued to tremble. Then he ran a handkerchief over his perspiring forehead. He looked over the two sheets, and reread the arithmetic problem. A parallelepiped – what the devil was that? Two minutes earlier, he had known perfectly well, but now it had gone out of his head completely. The tap whose flow sufficed to fill two-fifths of the basin filled him with confusion. What could be meant by two-fifths of a parallelepiped? And what about the other tap, which poured in water continuously?

His head was empty, as he looked again at the theme for a composition. What was an event? What events had he witnessed, and how could he tell the story of any of them? He thought back to his night school classes and tried to fish out of his memory some of all that he had heard there in the last three and a half months. But not a single word could he recapture. Then he thought of his wife and son waiting for him outside, and there was an ache in his heart.

The three examiners sat around a table at the far end of the room, as stiff as statues. Peppone wiped the perspiration off his brow. The clock in the church tower rang ten. How perfectly terrible! He looked out the window to make sure he had heard correctly. Yes, the hands were pointing to ten, and so were those of the clock in the schoolroom. He had barely written down the questions, and it was ten o'clock already. And those damned taps were still pouring water into that damned parallelepiped!

The old charwoman brought the news to the rectory.

'Father, I saw him with my own eyes. He's been staring for a whole hour and a half at the paper, and perspiring as if he had a high fever. Not a single word has he written!'

Don Camillo listened to her with satisfaction.

'That's what he gets for being so stuck-up,' he exclaimed.

'He looked just like a schoolboy,' the old gossip continued. 'He came up the road alone, but he got his wife and son to walk along parallel to him, behind the hedge. They met him at the schoolhouse door and waved good-bye.'

With that the charwoman went away, promising to come back later. She came at eleven o'clock, even more excited than before.

'Things are still exactly the same,' she reported. 'He's still perspiring, and still staring at the paper. In two more hours, time will be up. His wife and child are still hiding behind the hedge. She's chewed up half a handkerchief, she's so nervous. Father, I only wish you could see the state that big bully is in now!'

And Don Camillo thought he had every right to see the big bully brought so low.

The two strokes of half past eleven rang out, and Peppone was thinking that he had only an hour and a half more. Just then the charwoman came to call the director. The director went out into the hall and met Don Camillo.

'Excuse me,' said the priest, 'but even if the mayor is playing schoolboy he can't neglect his municipal duties. There's a poor woman who may die if he doesn't sign the papers authorizing her immediate removal to a city hospital.' And he held out a sheet of paper, adding: 'Will you give it to him?'

'That's not regular,' the director stammered.

'I know, but it would be still more irregular for a

poor woman to die simply in order not to disturb an examination. I don't think this will upset your examinee.'

The director shrugged his shoulders.

'Father,' he said in a low voice, 'it's positively nerve-wracking: all he's done is perspire!'

Don Camillo smiled.

'All these boys are the same way. Outside school they go in for a lot of big talk, but in class ...'

The director took the sheet of paper and started to go back into the classroom. Then he changed his mind.

'Father, I'll send him out here and let you give it to him in person. I'll leave the door open.'

Don Camillo glimpsed the sad state of Peppone and calmly waited for him. Meanwhile after Peppone had heard what the director had to say, he slowly got up and came out into the hall.

'Forgive me, Mr Mayor,' said Don Camillo, 'but it's an urgent matter.'

Peppone took the sheet of paper and read: 'I, Angiolina Pateri, widow, without means of support, state as follows ...'

'I've already told you that I can't do anything for her,' he said, handing the paper back to Don Camillo. 'I had this same statement in my hands two weeks ago.'

'Two weeks ago, things were different,' Don Camillo shot back at him. 'Please read on. Here you have the notarized signature of the doctor.'

Just then the director came out into the hall again.

'Mr Mayor,' he said, 'since you're called upon to decide an important matter, this time won't be counted. The commission has noted the exact hour at which you left the room.'

'Thank you,' said Don Camillo. 'I shouldn't want to have on my conscience the theft of time from a mathematics exercise or a literary masterpiece.'

Peppone gritted his teeth and shot a bitter glance at Don Camillo.

'Come, Mr Mayor, hurry!'

Peppone reopened the paper and scrutinized the declaration: 'The undersigned certifies that Angiolina Pateri is in a desperate condition and must be sent away for a surgical intervention; *meanwhile, ten minutes from now, you ask for permission to go to the toilet.*'

He reread the last two lines, fearing that he had misunderstood them. Then he looked at Don Camillo and asked:

'Why?'

'If the doctor says so, then it's got to be done,' answered Don Camillo. 'Just sign here.'

Peppone signed the paper and handed it back. When he returned to the classroom the commission took note of the hour. Don Camillo thanked the director and then said to him in a whisper: 'He may not seem to be so very bright, but you'll see. He's a slow starter.'

'Very slow indeed, Father,' said the director with a low laugh.

Ten minutes went by, and then suddenly Peppone raised the thumb and forefinger of his right hand.

'Go right ahead,' said the director. 'And smoke a cigarette while you're there, if you want to. We'll subtract the time.'

Peppone walked unsteadily to the toilet, which was at the end of a long hall. A window looked out over some empty fields.

'Psss!'

Peppone nailed his face to the grating over the window. Just below there was a pile of dried grass and sticks, and this was the source of the whistle.

'Hurry up, you jackass! Light a cigar and pretend to take it easy. Quick, tell me the problem!'

Peppone told him the problem between one puff of smoke and another.

'Parallelepiped . . . Basin . . . 40 by 60 centimetres . . .'

'What's 40 by 60 centimetres?' came the voice from outside.

'The base . . . two taps . . . one 8 litres a minute . . . other 5 litres every two minutes, but in 30 minutes fills two-fifths of the basin . . .'

'And what do they want to know?'

'How long it would take to fill the basin with both taps running. And the height of the parallelepiped.'

'Jackass! That's child's play.'

Don Camillo proceeded to explain it to him.

'Do you get it?' he said in conclusion.

'No, but now you've given me a hint, I'll try to think it out.'

'Beat it, then!'

Peppone jumped.

'How about the composition?'

'What's the theme?'

'An event which made a strong impression upon me.'

'Well, you'll have to work that out yourself. What do I know of your affairs?'

'But I can't remember a single thing! What shall I tell?'

From the pile of grass came a suggestion, and Peppone took it back with him to the classroom. He thought hard over what Don Camillo had told him about the arithmetic problem, and having caught on to the general idea he was able to work it out on paper. He was still perspiring, but in a different way. And the trembling of his hand was not the same, either. The director's voice aroused him:

'It's one o'clock and allowing you ten minutes for each of the two interruptions, you've only twenty minutes left.'

Peppone fell once more into a panic. Twenty minutes to make clean copies of both the problem and the composition! He looked around in search of help and his eye fell on the clock in the church tower.

'It isn't yet one o'clock,' he exclaimed. 'It's twenty minutes to.'

The examiners remarked that the hands of the classroom clock pointed to one.

'But I came with the tower clock and it's only fair that I leave by it too.'

'Very good,' said the director, who wanted above all to have everything proceed smoothly.

Peppone copied first the problem and then the composition, and when the tower clock pointed to one-eighteen he handed in both papers. Don Camillo was watching with a spyglass from the bell tower, and when he saw Peppone coming down the steps he adjusted the mechanism of the clock.

'Now try to catch up on those twenty minutes I set you back!' he murmured.

Looking again through his spyglass, he saw Peppone jump over the hedge and start home with his wife and son.

'Wretched creature!' the priest murmured. 'I wonder if at the oral examinations tomorrow, you'll find another shady character to help you the way I did today!'

But the next day Peppone did very well without any help whatsoever and the old woman teacher felt impelled to say:

'Allow me to congratulate you not only on your thorough preparation but on your good manners and sensitivity as well.'

Her fellow-examiner and the director both agreed, and Peppone went triumphantly home, not across the fields, this time, but down the street, with his head held high. Don Camillo sat in the church square, smoking his usual cigar butt, and Peppone marched decisively over to him.

'Did you get your diploma?' Don Camillo asked.

'Yes,' said Peppone gloomily. 'But you were your usual perfidious self to suggest "The Day of my First Communion" as subject for a composition. I was down and out, and you took advantage of me.'

'I can see that it puts you in real danger,' admitted Don Camillo. 'If Malenkov comes this way and this composition gets into his files, then you're done for! That's what you get for your pursuit of culture!'

As Don Camillo was passing in front of the main altar, Christ's voice stopped him.

'Where were you yesterday morning, Don Camillo?' Christ asked. 'You were away from here for some time.'

'Lord, please let it go by for the moment, will You? Later on we'll draw up accounts, and I'll pay what I have to pay.'

'You're shamefully lucky, Don Camillo,' Christ said with a sigh. 'Even when that time comes you'll find Someone to overlook what you owe Him and give you more credit.'

'Forgive us our debts as we forgive our debtors,' said Don Camillo, throwing out his arms. Then he remembered how Peppone's wife and child had waited for him behind the hedge.

'I did it for the sake of those two, Lord,' he said.

'For the sake of those three,' Christ corrected him.

'Oh well, one more or less doesn't matter,' concluded Don Camillo.

11 · THE STUFF FROM AMERICA

THE Party delegate was one of those gloomy, tight-lipped persons who seem to have been just made for wearing a red scarf round the neck and a tommy-gun slung from one shoulder. The reason for his visit to the village was to *galvanize* and *activate* the local section of the Party. He made endless speeches to the cell leaders, for when these gloomy tight-lipped fellows start talking politics they are as long-winded as the late Adolf Hitler. He stayed three whole days, and on the morning of the third day, when he had finished laying down the latest Party line, he said to Peppone:

'On Saturday you're to call a meeting of the village Council and announce that you're resigning from the post of Mayor.'

'Have I done so badly?' stammered Peppone.

'No, Comrade; you've done so well that you're to be promoted. You're to run for Parliament on the People's Front programme.'

'Me run for Parliament?'

'Yes, that's what I said.'

'But I haven't any education ...'

'You know how to obey, Comrade, don't you? All a deputy to Parliament needs to know is how to obey Party orders. And you're sure to attract votes. You're known all over the province for the way you hustle round and get things done.'

Peppone threw out his arms.

'But what about my own village?'

'Do you care more for the community than for Communism?'

Peppone bowed his head.

'Of course you'll have to make some campaign speeches. But we'll send you those, don't worry. You can just learn them by heart.'

While the delegate was giving him further instructions as to how to conduct his campaign, Smilzo burst breathlessly into the room.

'The stuff from America is here!' he shouted. 'I mean the foodstuff. There are posters up to announce that the needy can call at the presbytery for relief parcels. Spaghetti, tinned milk, preserves, butter, and sugar. The posters have created quite a sensation.'

'What's the exact wording of the announcement?' the delegate asked him.

'The fatherly heart of His Holiness ... etc ... etc. ... parcels which all the needy are entitled to receive upon application to the parish priest, Don Camillo ... etc ... etc ...'

'All the needy, did you say?'

'Yes, all of them, without distinction.'

Peppone clenched his fists.

'I knew that devil was cooking up something,' he said. 'They speculate in human misery, the filthy cowards. We'll have to deal with it somehow.'

'Yes, Comrade, deal with it!' the delegate ordered. 'Call a meeting of the cell leaders.'

When the cell leaders had hastened to answer the call, Peppone told them of the latest reactionary manoeuvre.

'Within half an hour the comrades must hear that if one of them accepts so much as a safety-pin I'll strangle him for it. Smilzo, you stand guard in front of the presbytery. Keep your eyes peeled every minute and take down the names of all those who go to pick up parcels.'

'Well spoken,' the delegate said approvingly. 'A case like this requires decisive action.'

All day long there was a line in front of the presbytery. The priest was jubilant, because the parcels were plentiful and well filled and people were happy to get them.

'Tell me if the so-called People's Party gives you anything better,' he said, laughing.

'They give nothing but tall talk,' everyone answered.

Some of the Reds were needy enough, but they didn't come. This was the only fly in the priest's ointment, because he had prepared a special homily for their benefit. 'You haven't any right to this, since you have Stalin to look after you. But take a parcel just the same, Comrade, and here's luck to you!' When none of the Reds put in an appearance and the priest was told that Smilzo was standing behind a bush, taking down the name of everyone that went away with a parcel, he realized that he would have to keep his homily to himself. By six o'clock in the evening all the 'regular' needy had been taken care of and there were left only the parcels for 'special cases'. Don Camillo went into the church to talk to the Lord.

'See here, Lord, what do You think of that?'

'I see, Don Camillo, and I must admit I find it touching. Those people are just as poor as the rest, but they're putting Party loyalty above their hunger. And so Don Camillo has lost a chance to deliver some sarcastic remarks at their expense.'

Don Camillo lowered his head.

'Christian charity doesn't mean giving the crumbs from your table to the poor; it means dividing with them something that you need yourself. When Saint Martin divided his cloak with a beggar, that was Christian charity. And even when you share your last crust of bread with a beggar, you mustn't behave as if you were throwing a bone to a dog. You must give humbly, and thank him for allowing you to have a part in his hunger. Today you simply aped the part of the altruist and the crumbs you distributed were from someone else's table. You had no merit. And instead of being humble, you had poison in your heart.'

Don Camillo shook his head. 'Lord,' he whispered, 'just send some of those poor Reds to me. I won't say a thing. I don't think I'd really have said anything before, either. You'd have shown me the light before I could say it.'

Then he went back to the presbytery and waited. After an hour had gone by, he closed the door and the front window. But after another hour he heard a knock at the door. The priest ran to open it, and there was Straziami, one of Peppone's most loyal followers, looking just as frowning and glum as ever. He stood silently at the entrance for a moment and then said:

'I don't think any better of you and your friends, and I intend to vote as I please. So don't pretend I misled you.'

The priest barely nodded. Then he took one of the remaining parcels out of the cupboard and handed it to him. Straziami took it and tucked it away under his coat.

'Tell me the truth, Father,' he said ironically. 'You might very well make a good joke out of the sight of Comrade Straziami sneaking in for a relief parcel from America.'

'Go out through the garden,' was all the priest said in reply, and he lit the butt of his cigar.

Peppone and the Party delegate were having supper when Smilzo came to report.

'It's quarter past eight, and the priest has gone to bed.'

'Is everything in good order?' asked Peppone.

'On the whole, yes,' Smilzo said with some hesitation.

'Speak up, Comrade,' said the delegate harshly. 'Tell us the entire story.'

'Well, all day long there was just the usual crowd, and I got all the names. Then just a quarter of an hour ago, a latecomer went into the rectory and it was too dark for me to see who he was.'

Peppone clenched his fists.

'Out with it, Smilzo! Who was he?'

'It looked like one of our people to me ...'

'Which one?'

'It looked like Straziami. But I can't swear to it.'

They finished their supper in silence, and then the delegate stood up. 'Let's investigate,' he said. 'Such things need prompt attention.'

Straziami's little boy was pale and thin, with big eyes and hair that tumbled over his forehead. Small for his age, he looked a lot and said little. Now he sat at the kitchen table and stared with wide-open eyes at his father, who was glumly opening a jar of fruit.

'That's for dessert,' said his mother. 'First have your spaghetti and tinned milk.'

She brought the bowl to the table and stirred its steaming contents, while Straziami went to sit down by the wall between the fireplace and the cupboard. From this vantage-point he gazed with a kind of wonder at his son, whose eyes roved in bewilderment from his mother's hands to the jar of fruit and then to the tin of milk on the table.

'Aren't you coming to supper?' the woman said to Straziami.

'I don't want anything to eat,' he mumbled.

She sat down opposite the boy and was just about to fill his plate with spaghetti when Peppone and the Party delegate threw open the door. The delegate looked at the spaghetti and examined the label on the milk and the jar of fruit.

'Where did you get this stuff?' he said harshly to Straziami, who had risen hesitatingly to his feet.

He waited in vain for an answer. Then he calmly gathered the four corners of the tablecloth into his hand, picked it up and threw it out of the window. The little boy trembled, holding both hands in front of his mouth and staring at the delegate with terror. The woman had taken refuge against the wall and Straziami stood in the middle of the room with his arms hanging at his sides, as if he had been turned into stone. The delegate closed the window, walked over to Straziami, and struck him across the face. A thread of blood trickled out of one corner of Straziami's mouth, but he did not move. The delegate went to the door and then turned round to say:

'That's Communism for you, Comrade. And if you don't like it, you can leave it.'

His voice aroused Peppone, who had been gaping from one corner of the room as if the whole thing were a dream. They walked away in silence through the dark countryside, and Peppone could hardly wait to get home. In front of the inn the delegate held out his hand.

'I'm leaving at five o'clock tomorrow morning,' he said. 'You've got everything straight, haven't you? On Saturday you resign and put Brusco in your place. You're to make your first speech at Castellino, and tomorrow you'll receive the main body of the text. You can insert references to local conditions in the blank spaces. Good night, Comrade.'

'Good night.'

Peppone went straight to Smilzo's.

'I'll beat him up,' he said to himself, but when he reached the door he hesitated and retraced his steps. He found himself in front of the presbytery, but there he did not linger either.

'That's Communism for you, Comrade. And if you don't like it, you can leave it.' The delegate's words were imprinted on his mind. At home he found his own son still awake in his crib, smiling and holding out his arms.

'Go to sleep,' Peppone said brusquely. He spoke in so harsh and threatening a voice that no one, not even himself, could have suspected that he was thinking of the wide-open eyes of Straziami's son.

In the room at the inn the Party delegate's mind was quite empty. He was fast asleep, satisfied with both himself and his Communism. But there was still a frown on his face, because Communists are on duty even when they are sleeping.

12 · A MATTER OF CONSCIENCE

FOR some time Peppone had been bringing the hammer down on the anvil, but no matter how accursedly hard he struck it, he could not get a certain tormenting thought out of his mind.

'The fool!' he mumbled to himself. 'He's going to make things worse!'

Just then he raised his eyes and saw the fool standing before him.

'You scared my boy,' Straziami said gloomily. 'He was restless all night long, and now he's in bed with fever.'

'It's your own fault,' said Peppone, hammering away, with his eyes on his work.

'Is it my fault that I'm poor?'

'You had orders, and Party orders have to be obeyed without discussion.'

'Hungry children come before the Party.'

'No, the Party comes before everything.'

Straziami took something out of his pocket and laid it on the anvil.

'I'm turning in my card. It doesn't stand for Party membership any more; it just means that I'm under special surveillance.'

'Straziami, I don't like your way of talking.'

'I'll talk as I choose. I won my freedom at the risk of my own skin, and I'm not going to give it up so lightly.'

Peppone put down the hammer and wiped his forehead with the back of one hand. Straziami was one of the old guard; they had fought side by side, sharing the same hunger and hope and despair.

'You're betraying the cause,' said Peppone.

'Isn't the cause freedom? If I give up my freedom, then I'm betraying the cause.'

'We'll have to throw you out, you know. You're not allowed to resign. If you turn in your card, you'll be thrown out.'

'I know it. And anyone that cheats too much is thrown out three months before he does it. To think that we have the face to call other people hypocrites! So long, Peppone. I'm sorry that you'll have to consider me your enemy when I'll still look on you as a friend.'

Peppone watched Straziami walk away. Then he took hold of himself, threw the hammer into the corner with a loud curse, and went to sit in the garden at the back of the workshop. He couldn't get used to the idea that Straziami had to be thrown out of the Party. Finally he jumped to his feet.

'It's all the fault of that damned priest,' he decided. 'Here's where I get him.'

The 'damned priest' was in the presbytery leafing through some old papers, when Peppone came in.

'I hope you're happy!' Peppone said angrily. 'At last you've managed to hurt one of our people.'

Don Camillo shot him a curious glance.

'Is the election affecting your mind?' he asked.

'Proud of yourself, aren't you? Just to have ruined a fellow's reputation, when this social system of yours has given him nothing but trouble.'

'Comrade Mayor, I still don't understand.'

'You'll understand well enough when I tell you that it's all your fault if Straziami is thrown out of the Party. You took advantage of the fact that he's so poor and lured him to accept a filthy food parcel from America. Our Party delegate got wind of it and caught him at his own house, red-handed. He threw the food out of the window and struck him across the face.'

It was clear that Peppone was highly excited.

'Calm yourself, Peppone,' said the priest.

'Calm yourself, my foot! If you'd seen Straziami's boy when the food was practically taken off his plate and he watched his father being struck, you wouldn't be calm. That is, not if you had any feelings.'

Don Camillo turned pale and got up. He asked Peppone to tell him again exactly what the Party delegate had done. Then Don Camillo shook an accusing finger in Peppone's face.

'You swindler!' he exclaimed.

'Swindler yourself, for trying to take advantage of poor people's hunger and get them to vote for you!'

Don Camillo picked up an iron poker standing up in one corner of the fireplace.

'If you open your mouth again, I'll slaughter you!' he shouted. 'I haven't speculated on anybody's starvation. I have food parcels to distribute and I haven't denied them to anyone. I'm interested in poor people's hunger, not their votes. You're the swindler! Because you have nothing to give away except printed papers full of lies, you won't let anyone have anything else. When somebody gives people things they need you accuse him of trying to buy votes, and if one of your followers accepts, you brand him as a traitor to the people. You're the traitor, I say, because you take away what someone else has given. So I was playing politics, was I? Making propaganda? Straziami's boy and the children of your other poor comrades who haven't the courage to come for food parcels don't know that they come from America. These children don't even know that there is such a place. All they know is that you're cheating them out of the food they need. You'd say that if a man sees that his children are hungry he's entitled to steal a crust of bread for them to eat, but you wouldn't let him take it from America. And all because the prestige of Russia might suffer! But tell me, what does Straziami's boy know about America and Russia? He was just about to tuck away the first square meal he's seen for some time when you snatched it out of his mouth. I say that you're the swindler.'

'I didn't say or do a thing.'

'You let another man do it. And then you stood by while he did something even worse, while he struck a father in the presence of his child. A child has complete confidence in his father; he thinks of him as all-powerful and untouchable. And you let that double-faced delegate destroy the only treasure of Straziami's unfortunate boy. How would you like it if I were to come to your house this evening and beat you in front of your son?'

Peppone shrugged his shoulders. 'You may as well get it out of your system,' he said.

'I will!' shouted Don Camillo, livid with rage. 'I'll get it out of my system, all right.' He grasped both ends of the poker, clenched his teeth and with a roar like a lion's bent it double.

'I can throw a noose around you and your friend Stalin as well,' he shouted. 'And after I've got you in it, I can pull it tight, too.'

Peppone watched him with considerable concern and made no comment. Then Don Camillo opened the cupboard and took out of it a parcel which he handed to Peppone.

'If you're not a complete idiot, take this to him. It doesn't come from America, or England, or even Portugal, for that matter. It's a gift of Divine Providence, which doesn't need anybody's vote to rule over the universe. If you want to, you can send for the rest of the parcels and distribute them yourself.'

'All right. I'll send Smilzo with the truck,' muttered Peppone, hiding the parcel under his coat. When he reached the door he turned round, laid the parcel on a chair, picked up the bent poker and tried to straighten it out.

'If you can do it, I'll vote for the "People's Front",' leered Don Camillo.

Peppone's effort made him red as a tomato. The bar would not return to its original shape, and he threw it down on the floor.

'We don't need your vote to win,' he said, picking up the parcel and going out.

Straziami was sitting in front of the fire reading the paper, with his little boy crouched beside him. Peppone walked in, put the parcel on the table, and untied it.

'This is for you,' he said to the boy, 'straight from the Almighty.' Then he handed something to Straziami: 'And here's something that belongs to you,' he added. 'You left it on my anvil.'

Straziami took his Party membership card and put it into his wallet.

'Is that from the Almighty too?' he asked. 'The Almighty sends us everything,' muttered Peppone, 'the good along with the bad. You can't ever tell who's going to get what. This time we're lucky.'

The little boy had jumped to his feet and was admiring the profusion of good things spilled out on the table.

'Don't worry; no one will take it away from you,' Peppone said reassuringly.

Smilzo came with the truck in the afternoon.

'The chief sent me to pick up some stuff,' he said to Don Camillo, who pointed out the parcels waiting stacked up for him in the hall.

When Smilzo came to pick up the last lot of them, Don Camillo followed him as he staggered under his loads and gave him a kick so hearty that both Smilzo and half of his parcels landed in the truck.

'Make a note of this along with the list of names you gave to the Party delegate,' Don Camillo explained.

'We'll settle with you on election day,' said Smilzo, extricating himself from the confusion. 'Your name is at the head of another list of ours.'

'Anything more I can do for you?'

'No. But I still don't understand. I've had the same treatment from Peppone and Straziami already, and all because I carried out an order.'

'Wrong orders shouldn't be carried out,' Don Camillo warned him.

'Right. But how can one know ahead of time that they're wrong?' asked Smilzo with a sigh.

13 · MADE IN U.S.S.R.

'Don Camillo,' said the old Bishop, 'your letter grieved me, not so much for what it said as for what I read between the lines. What is the meaning of your discouragement? Have you lost the faith that has been your bulwark for so long?'

'My faith is unaltered, Your Grace,' said Don Camillo sadly; 'it's a question of technique, of mechanics.'

And when the Bishop looked at him in astonishment he went on to say:

'The young people are getting away from me. It's as if they were racing off on motor-cycles and I were panting after them on foot. It's not faith that's lacking, but a motor-cycle.'

'That's not good reasoning, Don Camillo; it's a play on words.'

'Nevertheless, Your Grace, it reflects the true situation. I don't want to compete with the devil on his own ground; just because young people would rather dance than listen to my sermons, I shan't hold wild parties in the rectory. But because they are so dead set on the films, I want to show some that are a cut above the average. That's the point of what I'm trying to say.'

'How can that be the point, Don Camillo?' said the Bishop, throwing out his arms in bewilderment. 'Haven't you been putting on educational pictures for the last five or six years? What's so new about that?'

'The practice isn't new, Your Grace. And neither is the projector. It's an obsolete model, practically falling to pieces, and ...'

'That's quite enough, Don Camillo,' the Bishop interrupted. 'If the Good Lord lets obsolete models – such as myself – endure so long, it must be because they're still useful in one way or another. No, Don Camillo, you're trying to trick me. It's not true that you *need* a motor-cycle, you just wish you had one!'

But Don Camillo wasn't really trying to trick him. His 16-mm. projector was no longer a machine, it was the ghost of a machine that might have been. And a motor-cycle without a front wheel and saddle is a far less serviceable vehicle than shank's pony. Even the best film, when it came out of Don Camillo's projector, was a cinematographic omelette, and the sound-track was a cacophonic zigzag.

'The only thing I can suggest doing,' said the big-city repair-man to whom Don Camillo had taken it, 'is adding it to the rubbish, that is, if the Department of Sanitation will consent to take it!'

When he went back to the village Don Camillo was

strongly tempted to throw the thing in the river, but he could not give himself this satisfaction until he was sure of obtaining a replacement, or at least of obtaining the money with which to buy one.

In spite of his remonstrances, the old Bishop did not send Don Camillo away empty-handed. He gave him all the money he could, and although it wasn't very much, Don Camillo went home feeling happy. The first step was taken. There were thousands more steps to go before he reached his goal, but they did not weigh upon him. No landslide ever starts until the first pebble has fallen from the top of the mountain.

And so, after due time, came the promised day, and the arrival of the projector, a brand-new model with a sound-track as smooth as velvet. Don Camillo whitewashed the walls of the room and varnished the chairs. He rented a superlative film and posted announcements at every street corner. The afternoon before the great event he ran up and down the streets so often that inevitably he ran into Peppone.

'Is the mayor going to honour us with his presence tonight?' he asked. 'It's such a big occasion that our first citizen should really be on deck.'

'What big occasion do you mean?' asked Peppone in astonishment.

'The opening of the new picture palace.'

'I've never heard of any picture palace, old or new,' answered Peppone. 'All I know is that for some years past you've shown magic-lantern slides for the benefit of choir-boys.'

Don Camillo let this sarcasm go by.

'Let the dead bury their dead,' he suggested. 'We have a real hall and a fabulous new projector.'

'Fabulous as it may be, you're probably coming in on the last guard's van, as usual.'

'After you've been to one of our new shows, you'll see

that this guard's van is up at the head of the train and moving faster than even a diesel engine.'

'Fast or slow, the film is a superannuated medium,' said Peppone. 'It's dead as a door-nail, and there's no place for it outside a church hall.'

'What medium is in step with the times, then?' asked Don Camillo. 'The evening class in everyday revolution?'

'Leave politics out of it,' said Peppone. 'Progress has left the film behind. The coming thing is television.'

Just then Smilzo arrived upon the scene and threw out the question:

'Chief, what do you say? The expert is here and wants to know where to put the aerial.'

'Wherever he thinks best. I deal in combustion-engines, and television's not up my street.'

Smilzo hurried away, and after swallowing a lump in his throat, Don Camillo asked:

'Is our mayor a pioneer television owner?'

'Not myself personally, but the workers' Party, whose place is in the vanguard of progress. The T.V. set is for the People's Palace, and tonight is the first showing. But we shan't offer you any competition, Father. The set is a product of the State Radio Plant of Moscow, and only Party members are invited. I can't ask you to come, Father, much as I regret it, that is, unless you take out a membership card.'

'I admit that I'd like to see what this thing called television is all about,' said Don Camillo between clenched teeth, 'but I can wait a little bit longer.'

'*Fate vobis,*' said Peppone, throwing out his arms.

Don Camillo went home with a queasy feeling in his stomach and took his troubles to the Christ on the main altar.

'Lord,' he panted, 'Peppone and his gang have a T.V. set!'

'They're not the only ones in the world, are they?'

Christ answered. 'And it's not a death-dealing machine, is it?'

'They're not the only ones in the world, but they're the only ones in the village.'

'But why do you worry? Are you afraid that the appeal of something so new may lure some of your followers into the bear's lair?'

'No, only Party members can enjoy it. But I had hoped that my film hall would attract some of Peppone's hangers-on, and I could save them from the bear's embraces.'

Christ sighed.

'Are these your weapons, Don Camillo?' he asked. 'I didn't have any machines with which to seize men from the devil's grasp and put them on the path of righteousness.'

'Lord, forgive me,' said Don Camillo, humbly bowing his head. 'But the devil didn't have any machines then, either. If the devil rides a motor-cycle, why should I pursue him on foot?'

'Don Camillo, I can't follow your cycling metaphor. But the vehicles that carry men to heaven or hell are just the same now as they were then.'

The television set poisoned Don Camillo's entire evening, and in spite of the success of the film show, he was unable to sleep. Something about the affair was not clear in his mind, and the thought of this elusive, shadowy zone would not let him rest. The next morning, when he looked out of the window that gave on to the church square and saw the television aerial rising above the People's Palace, he was suddenly enlightened. That afternoon he managed to run into Peppone again and said to him brusquely:

'In this television business, are you following a directive from the higher echelons, or did you think it up yourself?'

'What do directives have to do with television?' asked Peppone. 'I do what I please.'

'Then you're a jackass, Peppone. Only a jackass could imagine that anyone in this village would take out membership in the Communist Party for the sake of seeing the idiocies projected by your teletrap, "made in U.S.S.R.". Who believes that they have television sets in Russia?'

'Oh, I forgot that in Russia they don't have either watches or bicycles!' said Peppone, throwing out his arms. 'According to you, this set of ours, which has "made in U.S.S.R." on every single part, is really a "product of U.S.A.", is that it? As you like! Those that have television can enjoy it, and the have-nots will just have to swallow their bile!'

Don Camillo's anger was plain to see, and he did well to go away without answering this last sally. When he reached the rectory he had to hear some first-hand reports on the village reaction to the new T.V.

'It seems to be positively wonderful.'

'And it was really made in Russia, so they say.'

'The Reds who went to the first showing are wild with joy. They say the Americans had better go and bury their heads in the sand.'

That night Don Camillo turned over and over in his bed, and his long quest for sleep was thwarted by the chatter of several noise-makers who wagged their tongues immediately under his window, on the church square.

'Too bad, though, that when they have colour T.V. we'll need a new set.'

'A new set? Not a bit of it! They haven't got colour at all in America, but in Russia they've had it for the last two years. And the sets made for export are geared to both black-and-white and colour. Did you see that red lever on the right side? You just pull it down, and there's the whole rainbow.'

'If I were Peppone, I'd put it on display at the Party's retail store, so that everybody could see. That way they'd stop saying that we keep it to ourselves because it's either home-grown or made in America.'

'Not on your life! They can say what they like, but if they want to see, they'll have to join the Party!'

Don Camillo was a captive audience. And when they stopped talking so loudly and began to laugh and whisper, he jumped out of bed and glued his ear to the aperture of the shutters.

'... a hall just as dismal as the other ...'

'... films more idiotic than ever ...'

'... and they say the sound is ear-splitting ...'

'... but what should he know about machines? They saw him coming ...'

'... you know what it is, when a man has a wad of money, whether it's a few liras more or less ...'

In order not to burst with rage, Don Camillo dived back into bed, where he didn't shut an eye before morning. But by the time morning came he had swallowed his anger and his brain was functioning in a normal manner. 'A canny player plays his cards close to the chest, and no one can guess what he has up his sleeve. If you're not showing your Soviet T.V. set, it's because the whole thing's a big story. You'll puncture your own balloon, if I give you time, Comrade Peppone!'

And so Don Camillo inaugurated a policy of complete indifference. When anyone spoke of the famous Russian T.V. set, he answered with a smile:

'If the Russians have the atomic bomb, why shouldn't they have T.V. sets and send them to their friends abroad?'

'What about the colour T.V.?'

'They've always been colourful! Why shouldn't they apply this quality to television?'

And so one, two, three months went by. Every evening there was a change of the guard at the People's

Palace, and a different group went to see the show, gathering afterwards below Don Camillo's window, on the church square, for an exchange of extravagantly laudatory impressions. Don Camillo was rudely awakened, and had to listen in grim silence. He held out for some time, but on perhaps the ninetieth occurrence it was too much for him to endure. 'Enough is enough!' he muttered to himself. 'I've taken all I can, God forgive me!'

This was ten days after the snowstorm which had caused the collapse of the roof of the People's Palace and the attic below. The roof and the attic ceiling had been promptly repaired, but the night watchman's quarters were still uninhabitable, because the walls had been soaked with water and the cement was not yet dry enough to permit removal of the scaffolding. The watchman, Lungo, and his wife and child were temporarily quartered elsewhere, and from midnight to four o'clock in the morning the People's Palace was empty.

One foggy evening a man went through the open door leading to the courtyard and climbed resolutely to the attic, where he lay for several hours in ambush. At midnight Lungo let down the iron curtain at the front of the retail store, gathered up the day's receipts and accounts, inspected the premises, locked the doors, and went to his mother-in-law's house. The intruder had such self-control that he waited two hours more before going into action. Slowly he made his way to the ground floor and the assembly hall. All the shutters were closed, and he was assured of complete privacy. With the aid of a torch he surveyed the scene. What he was looking for seemed to be veiled by a piece of cloth at the opposite end of the room. He walked over, removed the cloth, and gazed upon a shiny, new T.V. set, surmounted by a metal plate bearing the inscription 'Made in U.S.S.R.'. It wouldn't have been very hard to nail a plate of this kind on to a case containing an

American or British or Italian machine, and so the investigator detached the back cover. At this point his emotion was so great that he dropped the torch on to the floor.

'Lord,' panted Don Camillo, throwing himself on to his knees before the altar, 'something utterly astounding has happened. A fellow who accidentally got into the People's Palace last night took a look at the famous Russian T.V. set. And what do you think was inside the case? Nothing! Did you hear me? N-o-t-h-i-n-g! The case was empty!' And after wiping the perspiration from his brow he went on: 'Yes, Lord, empty! For ninety consecutive evenings those poor fools have taken turns going in groups to the People's Palace and then coming out to tell of the miraculous things they've seen. What colossal nerve, Lord! For three months no one has let the cat out of the bag. Just imagine the fun there'll be tomorrow, when the secret is known! The Russian T.V.! And yet I'll wager that if the discoverer doesn't tell his story they're quite capable of keeping up the farce indefinitely. Isn't it utterly ridiculous? Are they stark mad, to play a part like this, without ever giving themselves away? Self-discipline, they call it, but I have another name ... Lord, you aren't even listening ...'

'I was thinking of the sorrows of the world, Don Camillo, not of the tall tales you've been telling. What is it, then, that the visitor to the People's Palace saw?'

'Lord, a fellow accidentally got in there last night and saw the famous T.V. set,' said Don Camillo, hanging his head. 'It's authentically "made in U.S.S.R.".'

Don Camillo didn't breathe a word to a soul, but a week later when he ran into Peppone he couldn't resist remarking:

'Comrade, when will your faithful give up the game of the empty box?'

'When the time is ripe, Rev.!'

'Isn't it all very silly?'

'Just try getting up something equally silly among your highly respectable people!'

To this Don Camillo found no reply.

The next morning the village was startled by an amazing piece of news. A short circuit had caused the famous T.V. set to go up in flames.

'*But the enemies of the People have no cause to rejoice,*' said the poster which Peppone put up on the façade of the People's Palace. '*The working-class, no matter how ground down it may be, will have another T.V.!*'

They took up a collection, and ten days later the People's Palace no longer had an empty box; it had a box full of T.V.

'It's not nearly as good as the Russian set we had before,' proclaimed Peppone's henchmen, 'but it's better than nothing.'

And from their point of view, they weren't so very wrong.

14 · INFLATION IN THE PO VALLEY

THE question of television continued to be a sore point with Don Camillo, and smart salesmen have a way of sensing such things. The young man with the handsome tan brief-case was all smiles when he came to the rectory, insisting that all he wanted was to make the acquaintance of the most famous priest of the lower Po valley. Don Camillo still had some hundred jars of 'Atomic Floor Wax' in the basement, and he wasn't going to fall for sales talk, no matter how many blandishments went with it.

'Thanks for your kind words, but I really don't need a thing.'

'Father, you misunderstand me,' the young man protested. 'I'm no salesman, I work for Guardian ...'

'I see, it's life insurance ...'

'No, Father, you must be thinking of some other organization. Guardian Purchases is an entirely different matter, as you can see for yourself.'

These last words meant that he had managed to open his brief-case and put a dazzlingly illustrated catalogue into Don Camillo's hands.

'Motor-cycles, bicycles, cameras, typewriters, refrigerators, radio and television sets ... Guardian buys all these things direct from the makers at such a discount that it can make house-to-house sales on the instalment plan, with no increase over the list prices.'

Don Camillo tried to give back the catalogue, but the young man would have none of it.

'Don't worry, Father, I'm not here to sell. I only mean to give you an idea of all the lines we carry. If ever you want to buy any of these things, I'm sure you'll come to us. For instance, some day you'll surely get a television set, and it'll be worth your while to look over our large assortment ...'

The smiling salesman must have been Satan in disguise, or else how could he have known that Don Camillo was crazy to have a television set? But so far nothing serious had happened. Just to look at photographs of television sets didn't mean promising to buy one. The young man made this very clear.

'You have here an enormous range of models, from the cheapest to the most luxurious, all of them well-known makes. You can see for yourself that we charge the normal retail price, and the payments are extraordinarily easy. We call ourselves "Guardian Purchases" because our system actually guards and protects you. The debt you contract with us practically pays itself.'

Don Camillo was so taken with the television sets that

he forgot about the store of useless wax in the basement. But he did not forget that his personal finances were disastrously low. And so, after feasting his eyes on the catalogue, he insisted on returning it.

'I'll keep what you told me in mind,' he said by way of farewell.

'Thank you,' said the salesman, tucking it away in his brief-case. 'Just let me repeat that you needn't worry about the money. The day you decide to make your purchase just let me know and I'll come to write out the contract and pick up the initial payment. Of course, if here and now you happen to have as little as five thousand liras, it would be even simpler ...'

He must indeed have been Satan in disguise, or else how could he have known that, besides the burning desire for a television set, Don Camillo had exactly five thousand liras in his wallet? In any case, when he walked out of the rectory he had them in his pocket, together with a signed contract and a sheaf of promissory notes. Of course, he said that these notes were a mere formality and Don Camillo mustn't worry about meeting them. Don Camillo didn't worry. For some time he had warm feelings about the smiling young man, because the television set was a beauty and worked very well. But one day he found himself in trouble.

At the end of the fourth month Don Camillo couldn't meet the payment. The television set was his own personal luxury and he had to pay for it out of his own personal funds, which at this point were not merely low but virtually non-existent. Eighteen thousand liras aren't so very much, but if a poor country priest hasn't got them, what is he to do? He can't work overtime or give private instruction in the catechism. There was no excuse for appealing to his wealthier parishioners, for no object or institution of charity was involved. And no matter how poor he was, Don Camillo had his dignity. He couldn't borrow money to meet the payment due for a television set; after all, it was an extravagance and he ought never to have taken it if he didn't have extra means.

Finally he wrote to Guardian Purchases, but they wrote back that although they appreciated the unusual circumstances in which he found himself and were truly sorry, there was nothing they could do. The note had been sent to the bank and he must either pay up or submit to the bank's demand for payment. Complications increased, because Don Camillo was unable to pay the next instalment either. This time he did not have the nerve to write; he simply said a prayer and waited for pandemonium to break loose. The situation was particularly delicate for this reason. Although with time Don Camillo would doubtless have been able to restore his affairs to good order, a local election was at hand, and this was not the moment to have the bank publish his name. Don Camillo was not a candidate for office; he was not even enrolled in any political party. But the Christian Democrats' opponents were sure to seize any pretext for attacking a priest. Furthermore, to tell the truth, Don Camillo had been active in the last national election and the Christian Democrats had discussed their tactics with him. He broke out into cold perspiration at the thought of what Peppone and his gang would do if they had the bank's list of bad accounts in their hands.

After a number of sleepless nights and tormented days, the time for the bank bulletin's publication came round, and Don Camillo went all the way to the city to get a copy. Sure enough, the first thing he saw was his own name. He went back to the village in a state of great dismay and shut himself up in the rectory where nobody could see him. For he imagined that everyone must be in the know. That evening he ate no supper and could not even make up his mind to go to bed, but paced up and down the hall, with black thoughts crowding his mind. Peppone and his gang had acquired a formidable weapon against him, and he could just hear the accusations they would make in political meetings. His horror was all the more intense because he seemed to hear the crowd laughing. He must do something – anything – about it. And so, abruptly, he did.

Peppone was still hammering away in his workshop, and the sight of Don Camillo caused him to start.

'You must have something on your conscience,' said Don Camillo.

'A priest flitting about by night is bound to startle even an honest man,' said Peppone dryly. 'What do you want?'

There was no use making a short story long.

'I want to talk with you, man to man.'

'What about?'

'The promissory notes.'

Peppone threw his hammer into one corner.

'I have something to say, man to man, too,' he said. 'And I'd like to point out that, in spite of our enmity, I've never made political capital out of your personal misfortunes.'

'I can say the same thing,' said Don Camillo.

'I'm not so sure about that,' Peppone grumbled. 'But there's one thing that *is* sure: if you dare to be funny about my overdue note, I'll wring your neck.'

Don Camillo thought he must have misunderstood.

'What's your note got to do with it?' he asked.

Out of his pocket Peppone pulled a crumpled paper, which he thrust roughly at the priest.

'If you haven't seen or heard about it, you'll be sure to see or hear tomorrow. On the list of notes that have not been honoured there's one signed by your humble servant, Giuseppe Bottazzi.'

And there, under the letter *B*, was listed a note for twenty thousand liras in Peppone's name. Don Camillo had never noticed it simply because he was so intent upon looking for his own.

'Is that the only thing of interest you found?' he asked, shaking the bulletin in front of Peppone's nose.

'I confine myself to my own business,' said Peppone. 'I wanted to know if I was there, and there I was.'

Don Camillo put the bulletin into his hand, pointing to a certain line. Peppone read and re-read it, and then stared hard at Don Camillo.

'No!'

'Yes!' Don Camillo exclaimed. 'Devil take "Guardian Purchases"!'

Peppone started.

'"Guardian Purchases"? A most agreeable young fellow with a big tan brief-case?'

'Exactly.'

'And did you get a refrigerator, too?'

'No, a television set.'

Peppone launched into a tirade against instalment buying, an institution worse than the atomic bomb. Just a spot of cash and a trifle to pay every month, a debt that pays itself ... Then when you're unable to pay, you see that you were the trifler, and two hundred thousand liras of debt are ... two hundred thousand liras. Finally he calmed down.

'Well, since my refrigerator is working perfectly well, and you're in the same boat, there'll be no political consequences. Why worry? Don't you agree?'

'That's what I say,' said Don Camillo. Then a sudden thought caused him to turn pale.

'What about the third ticket?' he shouted.

The third ticket was a group of candidates put up by the Rightists, who were opposing both Peppone's Reds and the Christian Democrats' Shield and Cross. These candidates would have a cogent argument against both their adversaries, and the village would enjoy no end of laughter. Pietro Follini, the Rightist leader, was a fast thinker and an eloquent speaker. Peppone too turned pale.

'The idea that because of these filthy notes they may bracket me with the wearer of a clerical collar makes me see red!' he shouted.

'And the idea of being dragged down to the level of a godless fool makes me see black!' retorted Don Camillo.

They mulled it over for a quarter of an hour, and then Peppone pulled on his jacket and said:

'I'll go through the fields, and you go along the river. We'll have a showdown with that miserable Pietro Follini. First, you try to make him see reason. If he doesn't respond, I'll make him see stars.'

Follini had gone to bed, but he came downstairs when he heard Don Camillo calling. Great was his amazement when he saw Peppone beside him.

'Have you set up a common front?' he asked. 'I'm not surprised. Reds and clericals have the same end in view: dictatorship!'

'Follini, keep your wit for political meetings,' said Peppone. 'See if you can grasp what Don Camillo is going to tell you.'

They went to sit down in the parlour, and Don Camillo at once showed Follini the bank bulletin.

'Have you seen that?' he asked.

'Yes, I've seen it. I went to the city this morning for the express purpose of buying it. When I saw my name, I took it hard. But when I saw the names of the priest and the mayor, I felt better.'

Don Camillo took back the bulletin and thumbed nervously through it. Under the *F*'s there was Pietro Follini, listed as owing forty thousand liras. The three men looked at one another in silence, until Don Camillo said:

'I owe Guardian Purchases twenty thousand liras

for a television set; he owes them the same for a refrigerator. How about you?'

'I owe them forty thousand for a television set *and* a refrigerator. Both of them are working very well.'

'Same here!' said Peppone.

'Same here!' echoed Don Camillo.

Follini opened a bottle of wine. They drank together and before Don Camillo went back along the river he muttered:

'I'm glad there's not a fourth ticket!'

And before Peppone went back through the fields he mumbled:

'We're neatly matched. Television against television, refrigerator against refrigerator, and promissory note against promissory note! It's democracy in action!'

15 · GOLD FEVER

THE news exploded like a bomb around Monday noon, upon the arrival of the newspapers. Someone in the village had won ten million liras in the national soccer sweepstakes. The papers gave the name of the winner as Pepito Sbezzeguti, but no one in the town was known under such an exotic name. The bet collector, besieged by a curious mob, threw out his arms hopelessly.

'I sold any number of tickets to fellows from out of town at the market on Saturday,' he said. 'It must be one of them. Ten million liras! He's bound to show up.'

But no one showed up, and the village continued to fret, because they felt sure there was something fishy about the name. Sbezzeguti was plausible, someone of that name might have come to the market. But Pepito was going a little too far. Nobody who dealt in wheat, corn, hay, livestock and Parmesan cheese would be called Pepito.

'It's a phony name if you ask me,' said the proprietor of the Molinetto. 'And someone using a false name isn't likely to be a stranger. It must be a villager who doesn't want it known that he played the sweeps. Maybe he doesn't want his debtors to know, or his wife.'

The argument was logical enough. The villagers dropped the theory of the winner being an outsider and concentrated as intently as if they were trying to identify a common thief rather than the winner of a legitimate pool.

Don Camillo followed the affair less passionately but with a certain amount of interest. And because he felt that Christ did not altogether approve of his leanings towards the trade of a detective he offered Him an explanation.

'Lord, it's not a matter of idle curiosity; I'm doing my duty. A man who has received such a favour from Divine Providence has no right to hide it.'

'Don Camillo,' replied Christ, 'Divine Providence may take an interest in the soccer sweepstakes, although personally I doubt it, but surely not in all the publicity about the winnings. The fact of the matter is all that counts and it's quite adequately known. Someone has won a considerable sum of money, but why must you beat out your brains to discover his identity? Your business is to look after those who are less fortunate.'

But Don Camillo couldn't rid himself of his curiosity. The mystery of Pepito continued to occupy his mind until finally a great light dawned upon him. It was all he could do not to ring the church bells in exultation, and quite beyond his powers to resist putting on his cloak and going for a walk in the village. In time he arrived at the workshop of Peppone, mayor and blacksmith. Don Camillo stuck his head through the door and greeted his enemy.

'Good morning, Comrade Pepito!'

Peppone stopped hammering and stared at the priest in dismay.

'What do you mean, Father?'

'Nothing at all. Pepito's a diminutive of Peppone, after all, and by some strange chance Sbezzeguti is an imperfect anagram of Giuseppe Bottazzi.'

Peppone resumed his hammering.

Don Camillo shook his head.

'What a shame that you're not the Pepito who won the ten millions.'

'A shame, yes. In that case I'd be able to offer you two or three millions to go back home.'

'Don't worry, Peppone. I do favours for nothing,' said Don Camillo, going away.

Two hours later the whole village knew what is meant by an anagram, and in every house Pepito Sbezzeguti was vivisected to find out if Comrade Giuseppe Bottazzi was lurking inside. That same evening the Reds' general staff held a special meeting at the People's Palace.

'Chief,' said Smilzo, 'the reactionaries have gone back to their old tactics of smearing a good name. The whole village is in an uproar. They say you won the ten millions. There's no time to be lost; you must nail down their slander.'

Peppone threw out his arms.

'To say a fellow has won ten millions in the soccer sweepstake isn't slander. Slander means accusing someone of having done something dishonest, and the sweepstakes are quite on the level.'

'Chief, in politics to accuse someone of a good deed

is a smear. And an accusation that hurts the Party is definitely slanderous.'

'People are laughing behind our backs,' put in Brusco. 'We've got to shut them up.'

'We must print a poster!' Bigio exclaimed. 'We must come up with a statement that makes everything clear.'

Peppone shrugged his shoulders.

'We'll put our minds to it tomorrow,' he said.

Whereupon Smilzo pulled a sheet of paper out of his pocket.

'We've something ready, Chief, in order to save you the trouble. If you approve we'll print it right away and paste up the posters tomorrow morning.'

And he proceeded to read aloud:

The undersigned, Giuseppe Bottazzi, declares that he has no connection with the Pepito Sbezzeguti who won ten million liras in the soccer sweepstakes. It is useless for the reactionaries to accuse him of being a millionaire. All it proves is that they are a gang of neo-Fascists.

Giuseppe Bottazzi.

Peppone shook his head.

'It's all right,' he said, 'but until I see something in print I'm not going to rush into print myself with an answer.'

But Smilzo stuck to his argument.

'Why wait to shoot until someone has shot at you? Good strategy calls for beating the opponent to the draw.'

'Good strategy calls for a kick in the pants to anyone who sticks his nose into my private affairs. I can defend myself without help.'

Smilzo shrugged his shoulders.

'If you take it like that, there's nothing more to say.'

'That's how I do take it!' shouted Peppone, bringing his fist down on the table. 'Every man for himself, and the Party for the lot of us!'

The general staff went away grumbling.

'To let himself be accused of having won ten million is a sign of weakness,' observed Smilzo. 'And besides, there's the complication of the anagram.'

'Let's hope for the best,' sighed Bigio.

Soon enough the rumour appeared in print. The landowner's paper published an insert that said: '*Scratch a Peppone and you'll find a Pepito,*' and everyone in the village found this exceedingly clever and funny. The general staff held another meeting in the People's Palace and declared unanimously that something had to be done.

'Very good,' said Peppone. 'Go ahead and print the poster and paste it up.'

Smilzo made a bee-line for the printer's. Little more than an hour later the printer, Barchini, brought Don Camillo a copy of the proofs.

'This is bad business for the newspaper,' said Don Camillo sadly. 'If Peppone really did win the money I don't think he would put out such a statement. That is, unless he's already gone to the city to collect it or sent someone else to collect it for him.'

'He hasn't made a move,' Barchini assured him. 'Everyone in the village is on the alert.'

It was late, and Don Camillo went to bed. But at three o'clock in the morning he was awakened by the news of a visit from Peppone. Peppone sneaked in from the garden, and when he was in the hall he peered out anxiously through the half-closed door.

'Here's hoping no one has seen me,' he said. 'I feel as if I were being followed.'

Don Camillo glanced at him anxiously.

'You haven't gone crazy, have you?' he asked.

'No, no fear of that.'

Peppone sat down and wiped the perspiration from his brow.

'Am I talking to the parish priest or the village gossip?'

'That depends on what you came to say.'

'I came to see the priest.'

'The priest is listening,' said Don Camillo gravely.

Peppone twirled his hat between his fingers and then confessed:

'Father, I told a big lie. I *am* Pepito Sbezzeguti.'

For a moment Don Camillo was speechless.

'So you did win the millions, did you?' he said when he had recovered his aplomb. 'Why didn't you say so?'

'I'm not saying so. I was speaking to you as a priest, and you should have no concern with anything but the fact that I told a lie.'

But Don Camillo was concerned with the ten millions. He shot a withering look at Peppone and moved to the attack.

'Shame on you! A proletarian, a Party member winning ten million liras in a soccer sweepstake! Leave such shenanigans to the bourgeoisie! Communists earn their living by the sweat of their brow.'

'I'm in no mood for joking,' gasped Peppone.'Is it a crime to place a bet in the soccer sweepstake?'

'It's no joke,' said Don Camillo. 'I didn't say it was a crime. I said that a good Communist wouldn't do it.'

'Nonsense! Everybody does.'

'That's very bad. And all the worse for you because you're a leader of the class struggle. The soccer sweepstake is a diabolical capitalist weapon turned against the People. Very effective, and it costs the capitalists nothing. In fact, they stand to make money. No good Communist can fail to combat it.'

Peppone shrugged his shoulders in annoyance.

'Don't get excited, Comrade! It's all part of a vast conspiracy to persuade the proletariat to seek riches by other means than revolution. Of course that's pure fraud, and by abetting it you're betraying the cause of the People!'

Peppone waved his arms wildly.

'Father, let's leave politics out of it!'

'What's that, Comrade? Are you forgetful of the Revolution?'

Peppone stamped his feet, and Don Camillo smiled indulgently.

'I understand, Comrade,' he said, 'and I don't blame you. Better ten million liras today than the Revolution tomorrow!'

He went to poke up the fire and then turned around to look at Peppone.

'Did you come here just to tell me you'd won the money?'

Peppone was in a cold sweat.

'How can I get the cash without anyone's knowing?' he asked.

'Go for it, that's all.'

'I can't. They're watching me like hawks. And besides my denial is coming out tomorrow.'

'Then send a trusted comrade.'

'There's no one I can trust.'

'I don't know what to say,' said Don Camillo, shaking his head.

Peppone held out an envelope.

'You go for me, Father.'

He got up and went away, leaving Don Camillo to stare at the envelope.

The next morning Don Camillo set out for the city. Three days later he made his return. He arrived late in the evening, and before going to the rectory went to talk to the Christ over the altar. Opening up his suitcase he said sternly:

'Jesus, here are ten bundles, each one of them containing a hundred ten-thousand-lira notes. In other words, the ten million liras that belong to Peppone.

All I have to say is this: he doesn't deserve them.'

'Tell that to the sweepstake operators,' Christ replied.

Don Camillo took the suitcase away. When he reached the second floor of the rectory he switched the light on and off three times in succession as a signal to Peppone. Peppone replied by means of the light in his bedroom. Two hours later he arrived at the rectory, with his coat collar turned up to hide his face. He came in from the garden, through the door with the heavy padlock hanging from it.

'Well, then?' he said to Don Camillo, who was waiting in the pantry.

Don Camillo pointed at the suitcase, which was lying on the table, and Peppone approached it with trembling hands. When he saw the bundles of banknotes he broke into perspiration.

'Ten million?' he whispered questioningly.

'Ten million cold. Count them for yourself.'

'Oh no,' demurred Peppone, staring fascinatedly at the money.

'A pretty pile,' commented Don Camillo, 'at least for today. Who knows what it may be worth tomorrow? A single piece of bad news is enough to bring an inflation and turn it into worthless paper.'

'I ought to invest it right away,' said Peppone. 'With ten millions I could buy a farm, and land always has value.'

'It's the peasants that have a right to the land,' said Don Camillo. 'At least that's what the Communists say. They don't mention blacksmiths. They'll take it all away from you, you'll see. Communism is the wave of the future, Comrade ...'

Peppone was still staring at the banknotes.

'I have it!' he exclaimed. 'Gold! I'll buy gold and hide it away.'

'What good will it do you? If the Communists take

over, everything will come under the control of the State and your gold will lose its purchasing power.'

'I could always deposit it abroad.'

'Tut, tut! Like a regular capitalist! You'd deposit it in America, I suppose, because Europe is going Communist for sure. But when America is left out on a limb it will have to surrender to the Soviet Union.'

'America's got real power,' said Peppone. 'The Soviet will never take it over.'

'I wouldn't be so sure, Comrade.'

Peppone took a deep breath and sat down.

'My head's whirling, Father. Ten million liras.'

'Please oblige me by taking them home. But don't forget to send back my suitcase. That's my private property.'

'No, Father,' said Peppone. 'Keep the money for me, will you? I'd rather talk about it when I can think straight, perhaps tomorrow.'

After Peppone had gone away Don Camillo carried the suitcase up to his bedroom and went to bed. He was dead tired, but his sleep was interrupted at two o'clock in the morning by the reappearance of Peppone, together with his wife, both of them swathed in heavy coats.

'Forgive me, Father,' said Peppone. 'My wife just had to take a squint at the money.'

Don Camillo brought down the suitcase and deposited it on the pantry table. At the sight of the banknotes Peppone's wife turned deathly pale. Don Camillo waited patiently, then he closed the suitcase and escorted the two of them to the door.

'Try to get some sleep,' he said as they went away.

He tried to do the same thing himself, but an hour later he was once more awakened by Peppone.

'What's this?' he protested. 'Isn't the pilgrimage over?'

'I came to take the suitcase,' explained Peppone.

'Nothing doing! I've stowed it away in the attic and I have no intention of bringing it down. You can come back tomorrow. I'm cold and tired and entitled to my rest. Don't you trust me?'

'It's not a question of trust. What if something were to happen to you during the night? How could I prove that the money is mine?'

'Don't worry about that. The suitcase is locked and there's a tag with your name on it. I've thought of every contingency.'

'I appreciate that, Father. But the money's safer in my house.'

Don Camillo didn't like his tone of voice. And he changed his own to match it.

'What money are you talking about?'

'My own! The money you went to get for me in Rome.'

'You must be crazy, Peppone. I never got any of your money.'

'The ticket's in my name,' shouted Peppone. 'I'm Pepito Sbezzeguti.'

'It's plastered all over the walls that you're *not* Pepito Sbezzeguti.' You signed the statement yourself.'

'I am, though! Pepito Sbezzeguti is an anagram of Giuseppe Bottazzi.'

'No it isn't. It's an anagram of Giuseppe Bott*e*zzi. I have an uncle of that name and it's for him that I cashed in the ticket.'

With a trembling hand Peppone wrote *Pepito Sbezzeguti* on the margin of the newspaper lying on the table, and after it his real name.

'Damnation!' he exclaimed. 'I put an *e* for an *a*. But the money's mine.'

Don Camillo started up the stairs to his bedroom, with Peppone following after.

'Don't take it so hard, Comrade,' he called out as he climbed into bed. 'I won't steal your money. I'll use it for your own cause, for the cause of the downtrodden people.'

'Devil take the people!' Peppone shouted.

'You benighted reactionary!' said Don Camillo, pulling the sheet up over his head. 'Go away and let me sleep!'

'Give me my money, or I'll kill you like a dog!'

'Take the filthy stuff and go away!'

The suitcase was on the chest of drawers. Peppone seized it, hid it under his coat and ran down the stairs.

When Don Camillo heard the front door slam he gave a deep sigh.

'Lord,' he said sternly, 'why did you let him ruin his life by winning that money? He doesn't deserve such punishment.'

'First you scold me because he didn't deserve such a prize and now you call it a punishment! I can't seem to please you, Don Camillo!'

'I wasn't talking to you, Lord; I was talking to the sweepstake operators,' Don Camillo murmured as he finally fell asleep.

16 · A LESSON IN TACTICS

A MASSIVE piece of machinery distinctly resembling a car, with a 'U.S.A.' licence plate at the rear, drew up in front of the rectory, and a thin man, no longer young, but of erect and energetic bearing, got out and walked over to the door.

'Are you the parish priest?' he asked Don Camillo, who was sitting on a bench just outside, smoking his cigar.

'At your service,' said Don Camillo.

'I must talk to you,' said the stranger excitedly, stalking into the hall for all the world like a conqueror.

Don Camillo was momentarily taken aback, but when he saw that the stranger had reached a dead end and was about to descend into the cellar he moved to restrain him.

'This way!' he interjected.

'Everything's changed!' said the stranger. 'I don't get it.'

'Have you been here before, when things were differently arranged?' Don Camillo asked, leading him into the parlour, near the front door.

'No, I've never set foot in this house,' said the stranger, who was still in a state of agitation. 'But I still don't get it! Sermons won't cure the situation, Father. Nothing but a beating-up will teach those Reds a lesson.'

Don Camillo maintained an attitude of cautious reserve. The fellow might be an escaped lunatic, for all he knew. But when a lunatic travels in a car with a 'U.S.A.' licence and a liveried chauffeur, it is best to handle him with kid gloves. Meanwhile the stranger wiped his perspiring forehead and caught his breath. The priest scrutinized the somewhat hard lines of his face and tried to connect them with something in his memory, but to no avail.

'May I offer you some sort of refreshment?' he asked.

The stranger accepted a glass of water, and after he had gulped this down, apparently he felt a little calmer.

'You have no reason to know me,' he said. 'I come from Casalino.'

The priest scrutinized him again, this time mistrustfully. Now Don Camillo was a civilized man and one ready to acknowledge his own mistakes; he had plenty of common sense and a heart as big as a house. Nevertheless he divided mankind into three categories: good people who must be encouraged to stay good; sinners who may be persuaded to abandon their sin and, last of all, people from Casalino, a village which from time immemorial had feuded with his.

In ancient times the struggle between the two villages had been violent and men had lost their lives in it. For some years past it had degenerated into a cold war, but the substance of it was still the same. Politicians from Casalino had wormed their way into the provincial administrations and the national government, particularly the departments of public works and engineering. As a result, whenever there was any plan to do something for Don Camillo's village, these politicians blocked it or turned it to their own advantage.

So it was that although Don Camillo worked hard to keep good people good and to persuade sinners to abandon their sin, he left Casalino in God's care. When things got especially tense he would say to Christ, 'Lord, if You created these people, there must be some reason for it. We must accept them like death and taxes, with Christian resignation. May Your infinite wisdom rule over them and Your infinite kindness deliver us from their presence!'

'Yes, I'm from Casalino,' the stranger repeated. 'And if I have humiliated myself to the point of coming here, you can imagine that I must be very angry.'

This was easy enough to understand, but Don Camillo could not see the connection with the big American car.

'I was born in Casalino,' the stranger explained, 'and my name is Del Cantone. Until 1908, when I was twenty-five years old, I lived on a farm with my father and mother. We worked like dogs, because we had no peasants to help us. Then all of a sudden, those damned souls...'

He turned red in the face again and perspired profusely.

'What damned souls do you mean?' asked Don Camillo.

'If you, a priest, don't know that the Reds are damned souls, then you must be blind as a bat!' the stranger shouted.

'Excuse me,' said Don Camillo, 'but aren't you speaking of events of some forty years ago?'

'The Reds have been damned souls from the beginning, ever since Garibaldi invented that infernal red shirt...'

'I don't see much connection with Garibaldi,' demurred Don Camillo.

'You don't? Wasn't the doctor who introduced Socialism to this part of the world a follower of Garibaldi?' the stranger retorted. 'Didn't he put all sorts of ideas into people's heads and start subversive organizations?'

Don Camillo urged him to tell the rest of his own story.

'Well, in 1908 those damned souls made a big splash, with a farm-workers' strike and nonsense of that kind. They came to our place and insulted my father, and I took a shotgun and shot a couple of them down. No one was killed, but I had to run away to America. There I worked like a dog, too, but it took me a number of years to make any money. Meanwhile my father and mother died, in extreme poverty. All because of those damned souls...'

Don Camillo gently remarked that after all the shotgun was to blame. But the other paid no attention.

'When I heard about how Mussolini was taking care of the Red menace, I thought of coming back to settle my private account with them. But by that time, I was thoroughly tied up with a growing business. I did send someone to raise a gravestone to my parents in the cemetery. After that, more time went by, and now I'm in my seventies ... Anyhow, here I am, after four decades of absence. And I haven't much time. I came back to do something more to commemorate my father and mother. A gravestone is something as lifeless as those that lie beneath it. What I wanted to do was to give their name to some charitable institution, a fine, modern building with plenty of grounds around it. And my idea was to have the building divided in two parts: one a children's home and the other a home for old people. Old people and children could share the grounds and come to know one another. The end of life would be drawn close to the beginning. Don't you think it's a good idea?'

'Very good,' said Don Camillo. 'But the building and grounds aren't all that's necessary –'

'I didn't come all the way from America to learn anything so elementary. You don't think I imagine that an institution can live on air, do you? I meant to endow it with a thousand-acre, self-supporting farm. In fact, for the whole project I have put aside a million dollars. I haven't much longer to live and there are no children to inherit from me. Taxes and lawyers' fees will eat up most of what I leave behind. And so I transferred the million dollars to this, my native land. But now I've decided to take them back to America.'

Don Camillo forgot that the loss of this sum would be a loss to Casalino. In fact, with the notion of a million dollars earmarked for charity coursing through his mind he was willing to take the inhabitants of Casalino out of the category of untouchables and consider them in the same light as the rest of mankind.

'Impossible!' he exclaimed. 'God inspired you with a truly noble idea. You mustn't go back on His inspiration.'

'I'm taking the money home, I tell you,' the stranger shouted. 'Casalino shan't have a penny of it. I went there straight from Genoa, and what did I find? Red flags all over the village and on every haystack around!

Red flags, posters bearing the hammer and sickle and threatening death to this one and that. There was a rally in the public square and the loudspeakers brought me every word of it. "Now let us hear from our comrade the Mayor," they were saying. And when they saw my licence plate, they shouted at me: "Go back to Eisenhower! Go back to America!" One of them even damaged the top of my car. You can see for yourself if you don't believe me.'

Don Camillo looked out the window and saw that this was indeed true.

'Well, I'm going back, never fear,' concluded the stranger, 'and taking my money with me. I'll give it to the Society for the Prevention of Cruelty to Animals, rather than to the damned souls of Casalino!'

'But not all of them are Reds,' protested Don Camillo.

'They're all swine, though. The Reds because they're Reds, and the others because they're too weak to kick them out. Yes, I'm going back to America.'

Don Camillo thought it was pointless to argue. But he wondered why the old man had come to him with this story.

'I understand your disappointment,' he said. 'And I'm ready to do anything I can to help you.'

'Of course ... I had forgotten the most important thing of all,' said the stranger. 'I came to you for a very good reason. I've money to burn and expenses don't matter. I'm willing to make this my legal residence or do whatever else is necessary, to organize a secret raid and enlist the devil himself to carry it out. But my parents can't be at rest in the cemetery of Casalino, and I want to bring their bodies here. I'll erect a new gravestone in your cemetery, a monument of colossal proportions. All I ask is that you take care of the whole thing, I'm content to pay.'

And he deposited a pile of banknotes upon the table.

'Here's for your preliminary expenses,' he added.

'Very well,' said Don Camillo. 'I'll do whatever's possible.'

'You may be called upon to do the impossible,' said the stranger.

Now that he had got all this off his chest, he seemed to be in a more reasonable frame of mind. He consented to drink a glass of sparkling Lambrusco wine, which brought back memories of his youth and restored his serenity.

'How are things here, with you, Father?' he asked. 'Terrible, I suppose. I have an idea that the whole area is pretty much like Casalino.'

'No,' answered Don Camillo. 'Things are quite different here. There are Reds, of course, but they aren't on top of the heap.'

'Isn't your local government in Red hands?'

'No,' Don Camillo said shamelessly. 'They're on the village council, but not in the majority.'

'Wonderful!' exclaimed his visitor. 'How do you do it? You can't tell me that sermons have turned the tide.'

'There you're wrong,' said Don Camillo. 'My sermons aren't without effect. The rest is a matter of tactics.'

'What do you mean?'

'Well, it's hard to put into words, so I'll give you a concrete example.' And out of a drawer he took a pack of cards. 'Say each one of these cards is a Communist. Even a tiny child can tear them up one by one, whereas if they're all together it's almost impossible.'

'I see,' said the stranger. 'Your tactics are to divide your enemies and overcome them one by one.'

'No,' said Don Camillo; 'that's not it at all. My tactics are to let the enemy get into a solid block in order to size up their strength correctly. Then when they're all together, I go into action.'

So saying, he tore the pack of cards in two in his big, bare hands.

'Hooray!' the old man shouted enthusiastically. 'That's terrific! Will you give me that pack of cards with your autograph on one of them? The only trouble with such tactics is that they require unusually strong hands!'

'Strong hands aren't lacking,' said Don Camillo calmly. 'We can handle a pack easily enough. But what shall we do when there are sixty or more? We're still on top, but they're working day and night to put us down. And they have powerful weapons.'

'Weapons? And you haven't any? I'll send you plenty of those!'

'That's not the sort of weapons I mean. The Reds' chief weapon is other people's selfishness. People who are well off think only of holding on to their possessions; they show no concern for their neighbours. The richest people are often the more stingy; they fail to see that by clinging to their individual piles the whole lot of them will lose everything. But don't let's worry over that, Signor Del Cantone. Have another glass of wine.'

'There's the Old World for you!' sighed the stranger, turning down the offer of a second drink. 'I want to speak with the mayor right away. I see a way of killing three birds with one stone. I'll raise an enduring monument to my father and mother, save Western civilization, and madden those damned souls of Casalino by making this village the seat of my institution.'

Don Camillo saw stars. Then he hastily pulled himself together.

'The mayor's not here today. But I'll have him on deck here at the rectory tomorrow morning.'

'Good. I'll be here. Remember I have very little time, and be ready to present your choice of a location. I have the building plans in my pocket. And my agent has rounded up several big farms for raising all the produce the institution can consume.'

'No,' said Peppone, 'I won't take part in any such dirty comedy. I am what I am and I'm proud of it.'

'There's nothing dirty about it,' said Don Camillo. 'All you have to do is pretend to be a decent sort of person.'

'And there's no use your trying to be funny, either. I'm no puppet! I'll turn up at the rectory tomorrow morning, if you like, but with my red kerchief around my neck and three Party membership pins.'

'Then you may as well save yourself the trouble. I'll tell him to hang on to his million, because the mayor has no use for it. Our mayor intends to build a children's and old people's home with the funds they send him from Russia. In fact, I'll have the whole story put into print so that everyone can know.'

'That's blackmail!' said Peppone angrily.

'I'm only asking you to be quiet and let me do the talking. Politics shouldn't come into it. Here's a chance to do something for the poor, and we must make the best of it.'

'But it's a fraud!' said Peppone. 'Among other things, I have no intention of tricking that poor old man.'

'All right,' said Don Camillo, throwing out his arms. 'Instead of tricking a millionaire, let's trick the poor! To think that you claim to be fighting for a fairer distribution of rich people's money! Come, come! Is there any trickery in persuading a madman that you're not a Communist, in order to obtain funds for the needy? I see nothing wrong. Anyhow, I leave it up to the Last Judgement, and if I'm found guilty I shall pay. Meanwhile our old people and children will have shelter and a crust of bread. This madman wants to build something to commemorate his parents. Why shouldn't we help him?'

'No! I say it's dishonest and I won't have any part of it!'

'Very well,' said Don Camillo. 'You're sacrificing a cool million to Party pride. Perhaps tomorrow, when you're polishing up the weapons you've stowed away for the Revolution, a bomb will explode in your hands, leaving your son an orphan.'

'I hope you explode first,' retorted Peppone. 'And my son will never beg for your reactionary charity!'

'That's true. He'll have your pension from Malenkov. But what if you live long enough to achieve second childhood and there's no old people's home to take you in?'

'By that time Malenkov will have fixed things so that every old person has a home of his own.'

'What if Malenkov disappoints you?'

'I'm not worried about that. Meanwhile, I'll have nothing to do with this plan.'

'All right, Peppone. I have to admit that you're right. I was so carried away by the idea of doing something for the poor that I lost my head completely, and it took a hardened unbeliever like yourself to remind me of God's law against lying. It's never permissible to sacrifice principle to profit. Come along tomorrow morning, and we'll tell that madman the truth. I have sinned and it's up to me to atone.'

Don Camillo did not have the courage to speak to the Crucified Christ over the altar that evening. He slept uncomfortably and waited for the next morning to restore his peace of mind. Sure enough, the big American car pulled up in front of the rectory and the stranger walked in. Peppone, who was waiting outside with Brusco, Smilzo and Bigio, followed after.

'Here are the mayor and three members of the village council,' said Don Camillo.

'Good!' said the old man, shaking hands all round. 'I suppose that Don Camillo has already told you my story ...'

'Yes,' said Peppone.

'Splendid. I presume you belong to the clerical party.'

'No,' said Peppone.

'We're independents,' put in Smilzo.

'So much the better!' said the old man. 'I don't hold particularly with the priests. If you're free and independent, then of course you're against the Reds. Castor oil and a beating, those are the only treatments for them. Don't you agree?'

His slightly wild eyes were fastened upon Peppone.

'Yessir,' Peppone answered.

'Yessir,' echoed Bigio, Brusco and Smilzo.

'These cursed Reds ...' the old man continued, but Don Camillo broke in.

'No more!' he said firmly. 'This comedy has gone far enough.'

'Comedy? What comedy do you mean?' the old man asked in amazement.

'You were so excited when I saw you yesterday, that in order to calm you down I said some things that are not exactly true,' explained Don Camillo. 'Things are just the same here as they are at Casalino. The mayor and most of the members of the village council are Reds.'

'Did you want to make a fool of me?' the stranger asked with a grim laugh.

'No,' answered Peppone calmly. 'We simply wanted to help the poor. For their sake we were willing to stoop to almost anything.'

'And what about those famous tactics of yours?' the stranger said ironically to Don Camillo.

'They're still valid,' the priest answered determinedly.

'Then why don't you explain them to the mayor?' the old man asked vindictively.

Don Camillo gritted his teeth and took a pack of cards from a desk drawer.

'Look,' he said. 'Even a tiny child can tear them up one by one, whereas if they're all together it's almost impossible ...'

'Just a minute,' said Peppone. And taking the pack out of Don Camillo's hands he tore it in two with his own.

'Amazing!' exclaimed the old man. 'Record-breaking!' And he insisted that Peppone give him a split card with an autograph upon it.

'I'll display them both in the window of my shop in America,' he said, putting the whole pack in his pocket. 'On one side the priest's and on the other the mayor's. And in between their story. The fact that both of you can split a pack of cards is important,' he added. 'Likewise the fact that you can league together for the good of the village against an outsider. I still have the same low opinion of you cursed Reds. But I don't care if they burst with envy at Casalino; this is the place where I want to build my institution. Draw up a charter for it tomorrow and choose a board of directors with no politicians among them. All decisions made by this board must be approved by two presidents, who have a lifelong term and the power to choose their successors. The first two men to hold this office shall be Don Camillo and (if I have the name right) Giuseppe Bottazzi. Before we American businessmen embark upon any enterprise we obtain a thorough report on the people and places with which we expect to be concerned. Yesterday, when your priest told me that the local government was not predominantly Communist in character, I had a good laugh. Today I didn't find it quite so funny. But I have learned something I didn't know before and I shall go home happy. Push this thing through fast, because I want to settle it tomorrow. I'm buying the farm today.'

Don Camillo went to kneel before the Crucified Christ over the main altar.

'I'm not especially pleased with you, Don Camillo,' Christ said. 'The old man and Peppone and his friends behaved themselves more creditably than you did.'

'But if I hadn't stirred up the situation a bit, nothing would have come out of it,' protested Don Camillo weakly.

'That doesn't matter. Even if some good comes out of your evil-doing, you're responsible to God for what you did. Unless you understand this, you've misunderstood God's word completely.'

'God will forgive me,' murmured Don Camillo, lowering his head.

'No, Don Camillo, because when you think of all the good which your sin has done for the poor you won't ever honestly repent.'

Don Camillo threw out his arms and felt very sad, because he knew that Christ was quite right.

17 · CRIME AND PUNISHMENT

ON Easter morning, Don Camillo, leaving his home at an early hour, was confronted at the door of the presbytery by a colossal chocolate egg tied up with a handsome riband of red silk. Or, rather, by a formidable egg that resembled a chocolate one, but was merely a two-hundred-pound bomb shorn of its fins and painted a rich brown.

The war had not omitted to pass over Don Camillo's parish, and planes had visited it on more than one occasion, dropping bombs. A number of these had remained unexploded, half-buried in the ground or actually lying on the surface, since the planes had flown low. When all was over, a couple of engineers had arrived from somewhere or other, exploded the bombs lying far from any building, and dismantled those too close to occupied places. These they had collected to be disposed of later. One bomb had fallen upon the old mill, destroying the roof and remaining wedged between a wall and a main beam, and it had been left there because the house was derelict and the dismantled bomb no longer dangerous. It was this bomb that had been transformed into an Easter egg by unknown hands.

'Unknown', let us say, as a figure of speech, since there was the inscription: 'Happy Eester,' (with two e's) and there was also the red riband. The business had been carefully organized, because when Don Camillo turned his eyes away from the strange egg, he found the church square thronged with people. These scoundrels had all conspired to be present in order to enjoy Don Camillo's discomfiture.

Don Camillo felt annoyed and allowed himself to kick the object, which, naturally, remained immovable.

'It's pretty heavy!' someone shouted.

'Needs the bomb-removal squad!' suggested another voice.

There was a sound of sniggering.

'Try blessing it and see if it doesn't walk off of its own accord!' cried a third voice.

Don Camillo went pale and his knees began to tremble. Slowly he bent down and with his immense hands grasped the bomb at its two extremities. There was a deathly silence. The crowd gazed at Don Camillo, holding their breaths, their eyes staring in something akin to fear.

'Lord!' whispered Don Camillo desperately.

'Heave ho, Don Camillo!' replied a quiet voice that came from the high altar.

The bones of that great frame literally cracked. Slowly and implacably Don Camillo straightened his back with the enormous mass of iron welded to his hands. He stood for a moment contemplating the crowd and then he set out. Every step fell like a ton weight. He left the church square and step by step, slow and inexorable as Fate, Don Camillo crossed the big square. The crowd followed in silence, amazed. On reaching the far end of the square, opposite the Party headquarters, he stopped. And the crowd also stopped.

'Lord,' whispered Don Camillo desperately.

'Heave ho, Don Camillo!' came a rather anxious voice from the now-distant high altar of the church.

Don Camillo collected himself, then in one sudden movement he brought the great weight up to the level of his chest. Another effort and the bomb began slowly to rise higher, watched by the now-frightened crowd.

Now Don Camillo's arms were fully extended and the bomb poised above his head. For one moment he held it there, then he hurled it from him and it landed on the ground exactly in front of the door of the Party headquarters.

Don Camillo looked at the crowd: 'Returned to sender,' he observed in a ringing voice. 'Easter is spelt with an A. Correct and re-deliver.'

The crowd made way for him and Don Camillo returned triumphantly to the presbytery.

Peppone did not re-deliver the bomb. With two helpers he loaded it on to a cart and it was removed and thrown down a disused quarry at a distance from the village. The bomb rolled down a slope but did not reach the bottom, because it was arrested by a tree stump and remained wedged in an upright position.

Three days later it happened that a goat approached the quarry and discovered an alluring patch of fresh grass at the roots of the tree stump. In cropping the grass, it pushed the bomb which resumed its descent and, having travelled some two yards, struck a stone and exploded with terrific violence. In the village, at a considerable distance, the windows of thirty houses were shattered.

Peppone arrived at the presbytery a few moments later, gasping, and found Don Camillo going up-stairs.

'And to think,' groaned Peppone, 'that I spent an entire evening hammering at those fins!'

'And to think that I ...' moaned Don Camillo, and could get no further because he was visualizing the scene in the square.

'I'm going to bed ...' gasped Peppone.

'I was on my way there ...' gasped Don Camillo.

He had the crucifix from the high altar brought to him in his bedroom.

'Forgive me if I put You to this inconvenience,' murmured Don Camillo, whose temperature was raging, 'but I had to thank You on behalf of the whole village.'

'No need of that, Don Camillo,' replied the Lord with a smile. 'No need of that.'

One morning shortly after this, on leaving the house, Don Camillo discovered that during the night someone had defaced the white wall of the presbytery by writing upon it in red letters two feet high the words: *Don Camàlo,* which means stevedore, and undoubtedly referred to his recent feat of strength.

With a bucket of whitewash and a large brush Don Camillo set to work to efface the inscription, but in view of the fact that it was written in aniline red, the application of whitewash was completely useless and the letters only glared more balefully through any number of coats. Don Camillo had to resort to scraping, and the job took him quite half the day.

He made his appearance before the Lord above the altar as white as a miller all over but in a distinctly black frame of mind. 'If I can only find out who did it,' he said, 'I shall thrash him until my stick is worn away.'

'Don't be melodramatic, Don Camillo,' the Lord advised him. 'This is some urchin's doing. After all, no one has really insulted you.'

'Do you think it seemly to call a priest a stevedore?' protested Don Camillo. 'And then, it's the kind of nickname that, if people get hold of it, may stick to me all my life.'

'You've got broad shoulders, Don Camillo,' the Lord consoled him with a smile. 'I never had shoulders like yours and yet I bore the Cross without beating anybody.'

Don Camillo agreed that the Lord was in the right. But he was not satisfied, and that evening, instead of going to his bed, he took up his station in a strategic position and waited patiently. Towards two o'clock in the morning an individual made his appearance in the church square and, having placed a small pail on the ground beside him, set to work carefully upon the wall of the presbytery. But without giving him time even to complete the letter D, Don Camillo overturned the pail on his head and sent him flying with a terrific kick in the pants.

Aniline dye is an accursed thing, and Gigotto (one of Peppone's most valued henchmen), on receiving the baptism of red paint, remained for three days concealed in his house scrubbing his face with every conceivable concoction, after which he was compelled to go out and work. The facts had already become generally known and he found himself greeted with the nickname of 'Redskin'. Don Camillo fanned the flames until a day came when, returning from a visit to the doctor, he discovered too late that the handle of his front door had received a coating of red. Without uttering so much as one word, Don Camillo went and sought out Gigotto at the tavern and with a blow that was enough to blind an elephant liberally daubed his face with the paint collected from the door handle. Naturally, the occurrence immediately took on a political aspect and, in view of the fact that Gigotto was supported by half a dozen of his own party, Don Camillo was compelled to use a bench in self-defence.

The six routed by the bench were seething with fury. The tavern was in an uproar and the same evening some unknown person serenaded Don Camillo by throwing a firework in front of the presbytery door.

People were getting anxious and it needed but a spark to set fire to the tinder. And so, one fine morning, Don Camillo received an urgent summons to the town because the bishop wished to speak to him.

The bishop was old and bent, and in order to look Don Camillo in the face he had to raise his head considerably. 'Don Camillo,' said the bishop, 'you are not well. You need to spend a few months in a beautiful mountain village. Yes, yes; the parish priest at Puntarossa has died recently, and so we shall kill two birds with one stone; you will be able to reorganize the parish for me and at the same time you will re-establish your health. Then you will come back as fresh as a rose. You will be supplied by Don Pietro, a young man who will make no trouble for you. Are you pleased, Don Camillo?'

'No, Monsignore; but I shall leave as soon as Monsignore wishes.'

'Good,' replied the bishop. 'Your discipline is the more meritorious inasmuch as you accept without discussion my instructions to do something that is against your personal inclinations.'

'Monsignore, you will not be displeased if the people of my parish say that I have run away because I was afraid?'

'No,' replied the old man, smiling. 'Nobody on this earth could ever think that Don Camillo was afraid. Go with God, Don Camillo, and leave benches alone; they can never constitute a Christian argument.'

The news spread quickly in the village. Peppone had announced it in person at a special meeting. 'Don Camillo is going,' he proclaimed, 'transferred to some Godforsaken mountain village. He is leaving tomorrow afternoon at three o'clock.'

'Hurrah!' shouted the entire meeting. 'And may he croak when he gets there ...'

'All things considered, it's the best way out,' said Peppone. 'He was beginning to think he was the King and the Pope rolled into one, and if he had stayed here we should have had to give him a super dressing-down. This saves us the trouble.'

'And he should be left to slink away like a whipped cur,' howled Brusco. 'Make the village understand that there will be trouble for anyone who is seen about the church square from three to half past.'

The hour struck and Don Camillo went to say good-bye to the Lord above the altar. 'I wish I could have taken You with me,' sighed Don Camillo.

'I shall go with you just the same,' replied the Lord. 'Don't you worry.'

'Have I really done anything bad enough to deserve being sent away?' asked Don Camillo.

'Yes.'

'Then they really are all against me,' sighed Don Camillo.

'All of them,' replied the Lord. 'Even Don Camillo himself disapproves of what you have done.'

'That is true enough,' Don Camillo acknowledged. 'I could hit myself.'

'Keep your hands quiet, Don Camillo, and a pleasant journey to you.'

In a town fear can affect fifty per cent of the people, but in a village the percentage is doubled. The roads were deserted. Don Camillo climbed into the train, and when he watched his church tower disappear behind a clump of trees he felt very bitter indeed. 'Not even a dog has remembered me,' he sighed. 'It is obvious that I have failed in my duties and it is also obvious that I am a bad lot.'

The train was a slow one that stopped at every station, and it therefore stopped at Boschetto, a mere cluster of four houses three or four miles from Don Camillo's own village. And so, quite suddenly, Don Camillo found his compartment invaded; he was hustled to the window and found himself face to face with a sea of people who were clapping their hands and throwing flowers.

'Peppone's men had said that if anyone in the village showed up at your departure it meant a hiding,' the steward from Stradalunga was explaining, 'and so, in order to avoid trouble, we all came on here to say good-bye to you.'

Don Camillo was completely dazed and felt a humming in his ears, and when the train moved off the entire compartment was filled with flowers, bottles, bundles, and parcels of all sizes, while poultry with their legs tied together clucked and protested from the baggage nets overhead.

But there was still a thorn in his heart. 'And those others? They must really hate me to have done such a thing! It wasn't even enough for them to get me sent away!'

A quarter of an hour later the train stopped at Boscoplanche, the last station of the Commune. There Don

Camillo heard himself called by name, and going to the window beheld Mayor Peppone and his entire *giunta*. Mayor Peppone made the following speech:

'Before you leave the territory of the Commune, it seems to us proper to bring you the greetings of the population and good wishes for a rapid recovery, the which will enable a speedy return to your spiritual mission.'

Then, as the train began to move, Peppone took off his hat with a sweeping gesture and Don Camillo also removed his hat and remained standing at the window with it posed in the air like a statue of the Risorgimento.

The church at Puntarossa sat on the top of the mountain and looked like a picture postcard. When Don Camillo reached it he inhaled the pine-scented air deeply and exclaimed with satisfaction:

'A bit of rest up here will certainly do me good, the which will enable a speedy return to my spiritual mission.'

And he said it quite gravely, because to him that 'the which' was of more value than the sum of all Cicero's orations.

18 · RETURN TO THE FOLD

The priest who had been sent to supply the parish during Don Camillo's political convalescence was young and delicate. He knew his business and he spoke courteously, using lovely, polished phrases that appeared to be newly minted. Naturally, even though he knew that he was only in temporary occupation, this young priest established some small changes in the church such as any man feels to be necessary if he is to be tolerably at his ease in strange surroundings.

We are not making actual comparisons, but it is

much the same when a traveller goes to an hotel. Even if he is aware that he will remain there only for one night, he will be inclined to move a table from left to right and a chair from right to left, because each one of us has a strictly personal concept of aesthetic balance and colour and experiences discomfort on every occasion when, being at liberty to do so, he does not exert himself to create such harmony as he desires.

It therefore happened that on the first Sunday following the new priest's arrival the congregation noticed two important innovations: the great candlestick that supported the big paschal candle with its floral decorations and which had always stood on the second step at the Gospel side of the altar had been shifted to the Epistle side and placed in front of a small picture representing a saint – a picture which had previously not been there.

Out of curiosity, together with respect to the new parish priest, the entire village was present, with Peppone and his henchmen in the foremost ranks.

'Have you noticed,' muttered Brusco to Peppone with a stifled snigger, pointing out the candlestick, 'changes!'

'M-m-m,' mumbled Peppone irritably. And he remained irritable until the priest came down to the altar rails to make the customary address.

Then Peppone could bear no more, and just as the priest was about to begin, he detached himself from his companions, marched steadily towards the candlestick, grasped it firmly, carried it past the altar, and placed it in its old position upon the second step to the left. Then he returned to his seat in the front row and with knees wide apart and arms folded stared arrogantly straight into the eyes of the young priest.

'Well done!' murmured the entire congregation, not excepting Peppone's political opponents.

The young priest, who had stood open-mouthed

watching Peppone's behaviour, changed colour, stammered somehow through his brief address, and returned to the altar to complete his mass.

When he left the church he found Peppone waiting for him with his entire staff. The church square was crowded with silent and surly people.

'Listen here, Don – Don whatever you call yourself,' said Peppone in an aggressive voice, 'who is this new person whose picture you have hung on the pillar to the right of the altar?'

'Santa Rita da Cascia,' stammered the little priest.

'Then let me tell you that this village has no use for Santa Rita da Cascia or anything of the kind. Here everything is better left as it was before.'

The young priest spread out his arms. 'I think I am entitled ...' he began, but Peppone cut him short.

'Ah, so that's how you take it? Well, then let us speak clearly: this village has no use for a priest such as you.'

The young priest gasped. 'I cannot see that I have done anything ...'

'Then I'll tell you what you have done. You have committed an illegal action. You have attempted to change an order that the permanent priest of the parish had established in accordance with the will of the people.'

'Hurrah!' shouted the crowd, including the reactionaries.

The little priest attempted to smile. 'If that is all the trouble, everything shall be put back exactly as it was before. Isn't that the solution?'

'No,' thundered Peppone, flinging his hat behind him and placing his enormous fists on his hips.

'And may I be allowed to ask why?'

Peppone had reached the end of his supplies of diplomacy. 'Well,' he said, 'if you really want to know, it is not a solution because if I give you one on the jaw

I shall send you flying at least fifteen yards, while if it were the regular incumbent he wouldn't move so much as an inch!'

Peppone stopped short of explaining that in the event of his hitting Don Camillo once, the latter would have hit him half a dozen times in return. He left it at that, but his meaning was clear to all his hearers with the exception of the little priest, who stared at him in amazement.

'But, excuse me,' he murmured. 'Why should you have any wish to hit me?'

Peppone lost patience. 'Who in the world wants to hit you? There you are again, running down the left-wing parties! I used a figure of speech merely in order to explain our views. Is it likely that I should waste my time hitting a scrap of a priest like you!'

On hearing himself termed a 'scrap of a priest', the young man drew himself up to his full five feet four inches and his face grew purple till the very veins in his neck swelled.

'"Scrap of a priest" you may call me,' he cried in a shrill voice, 'but I was sent here by ecclesiastical authority and here I remain until ecclesiastical authority sees fit to remove me. In this church you have no authority at all! Santa Rita will stay where she is and, as for the candlestick, watch what I am going to do!'

He went into the church, grasped the candlestick firmly, and after a considerable struggle succeeded in removing it again to the Epistle side of the altar in front of the new picture.

'There!' he said triumphantly.

'Very well!' replied Peppone, who had observed his actions from the threshold of the church door. Then he turned to the crowd which stood in serried ranks in the church square, silent and surly, and shouted: 'The people will have something to say to this! To the town hall, all of you, and we will make a demonstration of protest.'

'Hurrah!' howled the crowd.

Peppone elbowed his way through them so that he could lead them, and they formed up behind him yelling and brandishing sticks. When they reached the town hall, the yells increased in volume, and Peppone yelled also, raising his fist and shaking it at the balcony of the council chamber.

'Peppone,' shouted Brusco in his ear, 'are you crazy? Stop yelling! Have you forgotten that you yourself are the mayor?'

'Hell! ...' exclaimed Peppone. 'When these accursed swine make me lose my head I remember nothing!' He ran upstairs and out on to the balcony, where he was cheered by the crowd including the reactionaries.

'Comrades, citizens,' shouted Peppone. 'We will not suffer this oppression that offends against our dignity as free men! We shall remain within the bounds of the law so long as may be possible, but we are going to get justice even if we must resort to gunfire! In the meantime I propose that a committee of my selection shall accompany me to the ecclesiastical authorities and impose in a democratic manner the desires of the people!'

'Hurrah!' yelled the crowd, completely indifferent to logic or syntax. 'Long live our Mayor Peppone!'

When Peppone and his committee stood before the bishop he had some difficulty in finding his voice, but at last he got going.

'Excellence,' he said, 'that priest that you have sent us is not worthy of the traditions of the leading parish of the district.'

The bishop raised his head in order to see the top of Peppone. 'Tell me now: what has he been doing?'

Peppone waved his arms. 'For the love of God! Doing? He hasn't done anything serious ... In fact, he hasn't done anything at all. The trouble is that ... Oh, well, Eminence, he's only a half man ... you know what I mean, a priestling; when the fellow is all dressed up – your Eminence must excuse me, but he looks like a coathanger loaded with three overcoats and a cloak!'

The old bishop nodded his head gravely. 'But do you,' he inquired very graciously, 'establish the merits of priests with a tape measure and a weighing machine?'

'No, Excellence,' replied Peppone. 'We aren't savages! But all the same, how shall I put it – even the eye needs some satisfaction, and in matters of religion it's the same as with a doctor, there's a lot to be said for personal sympathies and moral impressions!'

The old bishop sighed. 'Yes, yes. I understand perfectly. But all the same, my dear children, you had a parish priest who looked like a tower and you yourselves came and asked me to remove him!'

Peppone wrinkled his forehead. 'Monsignore,' he explained solemnly, 'it was a question of a *casus belli*, an affair *sui generis*, as they say. Because that man was a multiple offence in the way he exasperated us by his provocative and dictatorial poses.'

'I know, I know,' said the bishop. 'You told me all about it when you were here before, my son, and, as you see, I removed him. And that was precisely because I fully understood that I had to deal with an unworthy man ...'

'One moment, if you will excuse me,' Brusco interrupted. 'We never said that he was an unworthy man! ...'

'Well, well; if not "unworthy man",' continued the bishop, 'at any rate an unworthy priest inasmuch as ...'

'I beg your pardon,' said Peppone, interrupting him. 'We never suggested that as a priest he had failed in his duty. We only spoke of his serious defects, of his very serious misdeeds as a man.'

'Exactly,' agreed the old bishop. 'And as, unfortunately, the man and the priest are inseparable, and a man such as Don Camillo represents a danger to his neighbours, we are at this very moment considering the question of making his present appointment a permanent one. We will leave him where he is, among the goats at Puntarossa. Yes, we will leave him there, since it has not yet been decided whether he is to be allowed to continue in his functions or whether we shall suspend him *a divinis*. We will wait and see.'

Peppone turned to his committee and there was a moment's consultation, then he turned again to the bishop.

'Monsignore,' he said in a low voice, and he was sweating and had gone pale, as though he found difficulty in speaking audibly, 'if the ecclesiastical authority has its own reasons for doing such a thing, of course that is its own affair. Nevertheless, it is my duty to warn your Excellency that until our regular parish priest returns to us, not a soul will enter the church.'

The bishop raised his arms. 'But, my sons,' he exclaimed, 'do you realize the gravity of what you are saying? This is coercion!'

'No, Monsignore,' Peppone explained, 'we are coercing nobody, because we shall all remain quietly at home, and no law compels us to go to church. Our decision is simply a question of availing ourselves of democratic liberty. Because we are the only persons qualified to judge whether a priest suits us or not, since we have had to bear with him for nearly twenty years.'

'*Vox populi, vox Dei,*' sighed the old bishop. 'God's will be done. You can have your reprobate back if you want him. But don't come whining to me later on about his arrogance.'

Peppone laughed. 'Eminence! The rodomontades of a type such as Don Camillo don't really break any bones. We came here before merely as a matter of simple political and social precaution, so as to make sure that Redskin here didn't lose his head and throw a bomb at him.'

'Redskin yourself!' retorted the indignant Gigotto, whose face Don Camillo had dyed with aniline red and whose head had come in contact with Don Camillo's bench. 'I never meant to throw any bombs. I simply threw a firework in front of his house to make him realize that I wasn't standing for being knocked on the head even by the reverend parish priest in person.'

'Ah! Then it was you, my son, who threw the firework?' inquired the old bishop indifferently.

'Well, Excellence,' mumbled Gigotto, 'you know how it is. When one has been hit on the head with a bench one may easily go a bit too far in retaliation.'

'I understand perfectly,' replied the bishop, who was old and knew how to take people in the right way.

Don Camillo returned ten days later.

'How are you?' inquired Peppone, meeting him just as he was leaving the station. 'Did you have a pleasant holiday?'

'Well, it was a bit dreary up there. Luckily, I took my pack of cards with me and worked off my restlessness playing patience,' replied Don Camillo. He pulled a pack of cards from his pocket. 'Look,' he said. 'But now I shan't need them any more.' And delicately, with a smile, he tore the pack in two as though it were a slice of bread.

'We are getting old, Mr Mayor,' sighed Don Camillo.

'To hell with you and with those who sent you back here!' muttered Peppone, turning away, the picture of gloom.

Don Camillo had a lot to tell the Lord above the

altar. Then at the end of their gossip he inquired, with an assumption of indifference:

'What kind of a fellow was my supply?'

'A nice lad, cultured and with a nice nature. When anyone did him a good turn, he didn't bait them by tearing up a pack of cards under their noses.'

'Lord!' exclaimed Don Camillo, raising his arms. 'I don't suppose anyone here ever did him a good turn, anyway. And then there are people who have to be thanked like that. I'll bet You that now Peppone is saying to his gang: "And he tore the whole pack across, zip, the misbegotten son of an ape!' And he is thoroughly enjoying saying it! Shall we have a wager?'

'No,' said the Lord with a sigh; 'because that is exactly what Peppone is saying at this moment.'

19 · THE PRODIGAL SON

ONE day Don Camillo was in the church talking things over with the Lord, and at a certain point he said:

'Lord, too many things in this world are out of joint.'

'I don't see it that way,' the Lord answered. 'Man may be out of joint, but the rest of the universe works pretty well.'

Don Camillo paced up and down and then stopped again in front of the altar.

'Lord,' he said, 'if I were to start counting: one, two, three, four, five, six, seven, and count for a million years, should I ever come to a point where there are no more numbers?'

'Never,' said the Lord. 'You remind me of the man who drew a big circle on the ground and began to walk round it, saying: "I want to see how long it will take me to get to the end." So I must tell you: "No, you'd never come to such a point." '

In his imagination, Don Camillo was walking round the circle and feeling the breathlessness that must stem from a first glance into infinity.

'I still say that numbers must be finite,' he insisted. 'Only God is infinite and eternal, and numbers can't claim to have the attributes of God.'

'What have you got against numbers?' the Lord asked him.

'Why, that numbers are what have put men out of joint. Having discovered numbers, they've proceeded to deify them.'

When Don Camillo got an idea into his head, there was no easy exit for it. He locked the main door of the church for the night, paced up and down again, and then came back to the altar.

'Perhaps, Lord, men's reliance upon the magic of numbers is just a desperate attempt to justify their existence as thinking beings.' He remained uneasily silent for a minute and then went on: 'Lord, are ideas finite? Are there new ideas in reserve or have men thought of everything there is to be thought?'

'Don Camillo, what do you mean by ideas?'

'As a poor country priest, all I can say is that ideas are lamps shining through the night of human ignorance and lighting up some new aspect of the greatness of the Creator.'

The Lord was touched.

'Poor country priest,' He said, 'you're not so far from right. Once a hundred men were shut into an enormous dark room, each one of them with an unlit lamp. One of them managed to light his lamp, and so they could all see one another and get to know one another. As the rest lit their lamps, more and more of the objects around them came into view, until finally everything in the room stood out as good and beautiful. Now, follow me closely, Don Camillo. There were a hundred lamps, only one idea; yet it took the light of all the lamps to reveal the details of everything in the room. Every flame was the hundredth part of one great idea, one great light, the idea of the existence and majesty of the Creator. It was as if a man had broken a statuette into a hundred pieces and given one piece to each of a hundred men. The hundred men groped for one another and tried to fit the fragments together, making thousands of misshapen figures until at last they joined them properly. I repeat, Don Camillo, that every man lit his own lamp and the light of the hundred lamps together was Truth and Revelation. This should have satisfied them. But each man thought that the beauty of the objects he saw around him was due to the light of his own lamp, which had brought them out of the darkness. Some men stopped to worship their own lamps, and others wandered off in various directions, until the great light was broken up into a hundred flames, each one of which could illuminate only a fraction of the truth. And so you see, Don Camillo, that the hundred lamps must come together again in order to find the true light. Today men wander mistrustfully about, each one in the light of his own lamp, with an area of melancholy darkness all around him, clinging to the slightest detail of whatever object he can illuminate by himself. And so I say that ideas do not exist; there is only one Idea, one Truth with a hundred facets. Ideas are neither finite nor finished, because there is only this one and eternal Idea. But men must join their fellows again like those in the enormous room.'

Don Camillo threw out his arms.

'There's no going back,' he sighed. 'Today men use the oil of their lamps to grease their filthy machines and machine-guns.'

'In the Kingdom of Heaven,' the Lord said, 'oil is so bountiful it runs in rivers.'

In the presbytery Don Camillo found Brusco waiting. Brusco was Peppone's right-hand man, a big fellow who opened his mouth only when he had something important to say. His daily average of spoken words was perhaps the lowest in the village.

'Somebody must be dead. Who is it?' Don Camillo asked him.

'Nobody. But I'm in trouble.'

'Did you kill somebody by mistake?'

'No, it's about my son.'

'Which one? Giuseppe?'

'No, none of the eight that are here at home. The one that's been in Sicily all these years.'

Don Camillo remembered that in 1938 one of Brusco's sisters, who had married a man with land holdings in Sicily, had come to visit him. Before going she had lined up Brusco's nine children.

'Can I have one?' she asked him.

'Take whichever one you like best.'

'I'll take the least dirty of the lot.'

And her choice fell upon Cecotto, who happened to have just washed his face. He was about eight years old and somehow different from the rest.

'Let's be quite frank if we want to stay friends,' said Brusco's sister. 'I'll take him and bring him up and you'll never see him again.'

Brusco's wife had just died, and to be relieved of responsibility for one of his nine children was a blessing from Heaven. He nodded assent and only when his sister was at the door did he tug at her sleeve and say:

'Do you mind taking Giuseppe instead?'

'I wouldn't have him even as a gift,' she answered, as if she had paid hard cash for Cecotto.

Don Camillo remembered the whole story.

'Well then?' he asked.

'I haven't seen him for twelve years,' said Brusco, 'but he's always written to me, and now he says he's coming home for a visit.'

Don Camillo looked at him hard.

'Brusco, has the Five-year Plan gone to your head? Is it such a misfortune to see your son? Are you Reds ashamed of your own children?'

'No, I'm not ashamed even of Giuseppe, who's one of the biggest cowards I've ever known. It's my fault, not his, if he's turned out the way he has. This is an entirely different matter. In Sicily they're all reactionaries of one kind or another: barons, landowners, priests and so on. Of course, a son's a son, no matter what he does. But if he comes here I'll fall into disgrace with the Party. I should have let the Party know about the whole situation ...'

Don Camillo could hold himself back no longer.

'Come on and let the cat out of the bag!' he exclaimed. 'What has the poor fellow done?'

Brusco lowered his head.

'They sent him to school ...' he muttered.

'Well, you're not ashamed of him for that, are you?'

'No, but he's studying for the priesthood.'

Don Camillo couldn't help laughing.

'So your son's a priest! That's a good one! A priest!'

'Pretty nearly one ... But you needn't rub it in.'

Don Camillo had never heard Brusco speak in just this tone of voice. He waited to hear more.

'If he comes here, and Peppone catches on, he'll kill me. And since the boy's a priest, or nearly, I don't want him to know that I'm on the other side. You priests understand one another. And if you can't think of something, I'm done for. He's arriving at eight o'clock tomorrow.'

'All right. Let me sleep on it.'

Brusco had never thanked anyone in his life.

'I'll make it up to you,' he muttered. And he added, from the door: 'I have the worst luck! With all the reactionaries there are around, why did I have to have a priest for a son?'

Don Camillo was not in the least discomfited.

'With all the rogues there are available, why should a poor priest be cursed with a Communist father?'

Brusco shook his head.

'Everyone has his own troubles,' he said with a bitter sigh.

20 · THUNDER

Two days before the opening of the hunting season, Lightning died. He was as old as the hills and had every reason to be sick and tired of playing the part of a hunting dog when he wasn't born one. Don Camillo could do nothing but dig a deep hole beside the acacia tree, toss in the body, and heave a long sigh. For a whole fortnight he was depressed, but finally he got over it, and one morning he found himself out in the fields with a shotgun in his hands. A quail rose out of a nearby meadow, and Don Camillo shot at him, but the quail flew on as calmly as before. Don Camillo nearly yelled, 'You wretched dog!' but he remembered that Lightning wasn't there, and felt depressed all over again. He wandered about the fields, over the river bank and under grape arbours, discharged as many volleys as a machine-gun, but never made a single hit. Who could be lucky without a dog beside him?

With the one cartridge he had left, he aimed at a quail flying low over a hedge. He couldn't have missed, but there was no way to be sure. The quail might have fallen either into the hedge or into the field on the other side. But to search for it would be like looking for a needle in a haystack. Better give the whole thing up. He blew into the barrels of his gun and was looking round to see where he was and which was the shortest way to go home when a rustle made him turn his head. Out of the hedge jumped a dog, holding a hare in his mouth, which he proceeded to drop at Don Camillo's feet.

He picked the hare up and found that it was soaking wet, and so was the dog. Obviously he had swum across from the opposite side of the river. Don Camillo slipped the hare into his bag and started home, with the dog following. When he reached the presbytery, the dog crouched outside the door. Don Camillo had never seen a dog like him. He was a fine animal and seemed to be in the pink of condition. Perhaps he was a dog with a pedigree like that of a count or a marquis, but he had no identification papers on him. He wore a handsome collar, but there was no plate or tag attached to it.

'If he doesn't come from another world but has a rightful owner in this one, surely someone will turn up to look for him,' Don Camillo thought to himself. And he let the dog in. That evening before going to bed, he thought about the dog, and finally put his conscience at rest by saying to himself: 'I'll mention him in church on Sunday.' The next morning, when he got up to say mass, he forgot all about the dog until he found him at the church door.

'Stay there and wait for me,' Don Camillo shouted.

And the dog curled up in front of the sacristy door, where after mass he gave the priest an enthusiastic greeting. They breakfasted together, and when the dog saw Don Camillo take his shotgun out of the corner where he had left it and hang it on a nail, he barked, ran to the door, returned to see if Don Camillo were following and, in short, would give him no peace until Don Camillo slung the gun over his shoulder and made for the fields. He was an extraordinary dog, one of the kind that puts a hunter on his mettle and makes him think: 'If I miss my aim, *I'm* a dirty dog.' Don Camillo concentrated as if he were under examination and showed himself to be a worthy master. On his way home with a bag full of game, he said to himself: 'I'll call him Thunder.' Now that the dog had done his work, he was amusing himself by chasing butterflies in a meadow.

'Thunder!' Don Camillo shouted.

It seemed as if from the far side of the meadow someone had launched a torpedo. The dog streaked along with his belly close to the ground, leaving the long grass parted in his wake. He arrived in front of Don Camillo with six inches of tongue hanging out, ready for orders.

'Good dog!' said Don Camillo, and Thunder danced and barked with such joy that Don Camillo thought 'If he doesn't leave off, I'll find myself dancing and barking.'

Two days went by, and Satan tagged at Don Camillo's heels, whispering to him that he should forget to say anything about the dog in church on Sunday. On the afternoon of the third day, when Don Camillo was on his way home with a bag of game and Thunder frisking ahead of him, he ran into Peppone. Peppone was in a gloomy mood; he had been hunting too, but his bag was empty. Now he looked at Thunder, took a newspaper out of his pocket and opened it.

'That's funny,' he said. 'He looks just like the dog they've advertised as lost.'

Don Camillo took the paper from him and found what he had hoped he would not find. Someone from the city was offering a reward to anyone who found a hunting dog with such and such marks upon him, lost three days before along the river.

'Very well, then,' said Don Camillo. 'I needn't make any announcement in church. Let me keep this paper. I'll give it back to you later.'

'It's really too bad,' said Peppone. 'Everyone says he's an extraordinary dog. And they must be right, because when you had Lightning you never brought home a haul like that one. If I were in your shoes ...'

'And if I were in yours ...' Don Camillo interrupted. 'But I happen to be in my own, and as an honest man I must restore the dog to his rightful owner.'

When they reached the village Don Camillo sent a telegram to the man in the city. Satan had been working out a new argument to use on Don Camillo, but he was too slow, because he had counted on Don Camillo's sending a letter rather than a telegram. That would have taken fifteen or twenty minutes, time enough for anyone so persuasive as Satan to win a point reluctantly defended. But a five-word telegram was so quickly dispatched that Satan was left at a standstill. Don Camillo went home with his conscience in good order, but with a feeling of deep depression. And he sighed even more deeply than when he had buried Lightning.

The city man drove up the next day in a low-slung sports model. He was vain and unpleasant, as might have been expected from his flashy taste in cars; what is called a city slicker.

'Where is my dog?' he asked.

'A dog has been found that must belong to somebody,' said Don Camillo. 'But you'll have to prove your ownership.'

The man described the dog from stem to stern.

'Is that enough?' he asked. 'Or do I have to describe his insides as well?'

'That's enough,' said Don Camillo glumly, opening the cellar door.

The dog lay on the floor without moving.

'Thunder!' called the city slicker.

'Is that really his name?' asked Don Camillo.

'Yes.'

'That's funny.'

Still the dog did not move and the man called again:

'Thunder!'

The dog growled and there was an ugly look in his eyes.

'He doesn't seem to be yours,' observed Don Camillo.

The claimant went and took the dog by the collar in order to drag him up from the cellar. Then he turned the collar inside out, revealing a brass plate with a name on it.

'Just read this, Father. Here are my name and address and telephone number. Appearances to the contrary, the dog is mine.'

Then he pointed to the car.

'Get in!' he ordered.

The dog obeyed, with his head hanging low and his tail between his legs, and curled up on the back seat. His owner held out a five-thousand lire note.

'Here's for your trouble,' he said.

'It's no trouble to restore something lost to its rightful owner,' said Don Camillo, proudly pushing the money away.

'I'm truly grateful,' said the city slicker. 'He's a very expensive dog, a thoroughbred from one of the best

English kennels, with three international blue ribbons to his credit. I'm an impulsive sort of fellow, and the other day, when he caused me to miss a hare, I gave him a kick. And he resented it.'

'He's a dog with professional dignity,' said Don Camillo. 'And you didn't miss the hare, because he brought it to me.'

'Oh well, he'll get over it,' said the city slicker, climbing back into his car.

Don Camillo spent a restless night, and when he got up to say mass the next morning he was immersed in gloom. It was windy and pouring rain, but Thunder was there. He was covered with mud and soaked like a sponge, but he lay in front of the sacristy door and gave Don Camillo a welcome worthy of the last act of an opera. Don Camillo went in and spoke to the Lord.

'Lord, Your enemies are going to say that Christians are afraid of wind and water, because not a single one of them has come to church this morning. But if You let Thunder in, they'll be confounded.'

Thunder was admitted to the sacristy, where he waited patiently, except when he stuck his nose through the door near the altar, causing Don Camillo to stumble over his prayers. They went back to the presbytery together, and the priest sank into his former melancholy.

'No use fooling myself,' he said with a sigh. 'He knows the way, and he'll come back for you.'

The dog growled as if he had understood. He let Don Camillo brush him and then sat down by the fire to dry. The owner returned in the afternoon. He was in a very bad humour, because he had got his car muddy. There was no need for explanations; he walked into the presbytery and found Thunder in front of the spent fire.

'Sorry to have given you more trouble,' he said, 'but

it won't happen again. I'll take him to a place of mine in the next province, and he couldn't find his way back from there even if he were a carrier pigeon.'

When his master called this time, Thunder gave an angry bark. He would not get into the car of his own accord, but had to be lifted on to the seat. He tried to escape, and when the door was closed he scratched and barked without ceasing.

The next morning Don Camillo left the presbytery with his heart pounding. Thunder was not there either that day or the next, and little by little the priest resigned himself to his absence. A fortnight went by, and on the fifteenth night, at about one o'clock, Don Camillo heard a cry from below and knew that it was Thunder. He ran downstairs and out on the church square, quite forgetting that he was in his nightshirt. Thunder was in a very bad condition: starved, dirty, and so tired that he could not hold up his tail. It took three days to restore him to normal, but on the fourth day, after mass, Thunder pulled him by his cassock to where the shotgun was hanging and made such a scene that Don Camillo took his gun, bag, and cartridge-belt and set out for the fields. There followed a rare and wonderful week, when Don Camillo's catches made the most seasoned hunters green with envy. Every now and then someone came to see the dog, and Don Camillo explained:

'He's not mine. A man from the city left him here to be trained to chase hares.'

One fine morning Peppone came to admire him. He stared at him for some time in silence.

'I'm not going to hunt this morning,' said Don Camillo. 'Do you want to try him?'

'Will he come?' said Peppone incredulously.

'I think he will. After all, he doesn't know you're a

Communist. Seeing you in my company, he probably takes you for a perfectly respectable person.'

Peppone was so absorbed by the prospect of trying the dog that he did not answer. Don Camillo turned his gun and bag and cartridge-belt over to Peppone. Thunder had been excited to see Don Camillo take down his gun, but now he seemed taken aback.

'Go along with the Mayor,' said Don Camillo. 'I'm busy today.'

Peppone put on the belt and hung the gun and bag over his shoulder. Thunder looked first at one man and then the other.

'Go on,' Don Camillo encouraged him. 'He's ugly, but he doesn't bite.'

Thunder started to follow Peppone, but then he stopped in perplexed fashion and turned round.

'Go, go,' Don Camillo repeated. 'Only watch out that he doesn't enlist you in the Party.'

Thunder went along. If Don Camillo had turned over his hunting equipment to this man, he must be a friend. Two hours later he bounded back into the presbytery and laid a magnificent hare at Don Camillo's feet. Soon, panting like a locomotive, Peppone arrived upon the scene.

'Devil take you and your dog!' he exclaimed. 'He's a perfect wonder, but he eats the game. He stole a hare a yard long. After he had brought me the quails and the partridges, he had to steal a hare.'

Don Camillo picked up the hare and held it out to Peppone.

'He's a thinking dog,' he answered. 'He thought that if the gun and the cartridges were mine, I was entitled to part of the kill.'

It was plain that Thunder had acted in good faith, because he had not run away from Peppone, but greeted him with affection.

'He's an extraordinary animal,' said Peppone, 'and I wouldn't give him back to that man even if he came with a regiment of militia.'

Don Camillo sighed.

The owner turned up a week later. He wore a hunting outfit and carried a feather-weight Belgian shotgun.

'Well, he got away from up there, too. I've come to see whether he landed here again.'

'He arrived yesterday morning,' said Don Camillo glumly. 'Take him away.'

Thunder looked at his master and growled.

'I'll settle accounts with you this time,' said the city slicker to the dog.

Thunder growled again, and the city slicker lost his head and gave him a kick.

'You cur! I'll teach you! Lie down!'

The dog lay down, growling, and Don Camillo stepped in.

'He's a thoroughbred, and you can't handle him with violence. Let him quieten down while you drink a glass of wine.'

The man took a seat, and Don Camillo went down to get a bottle from the cellar. While he was there he found time to scribble a note which he gave to the bell-ringer's son.

'Take it to Peppone at his workshop, and hurry.'

The note contained only a few words: *'The fellow's here again. Lend me twenty thousand lire so I can try to buy the dog. And get them here fast.'*

The city slicker drank several glasses of wine, talked idly to Don Camillo, then looked at his watch and stood up.

'I'm sorry, but I must go. Friends are expecting me for the hunt, and I've just time to get there.'

Thunder was still crouching in a corner, and as soon

as he saw his master looking at him he began to growl. He growled louder when the man came near. Just then there came the roar of a motor-cycle and Don Camillo saw Peppone dismount from it. He made an interrogative gesture and Peppone nodded an affirmative answer. He held up two open hands, then one, and finally one finger. Then with his right hand he made a horizontal cut through the air. Which signified that he had sixteen thousand five hundred lire. Don Camillo sighed with relief.

'Sir,' he said to the visitor. 'You can see that the dog has taken a dislike to you. Thoroughbreds don't forget, and you'll never make him put it behind him. Why don't you sell him to me?'

Then he made a mental calculation of all his resources.

'I can pay you eighteen thousand eight hundred lire. That's all I possess.'

The city slicker sneered.

'Father, you must be joking. The dog cost me eighty thousand and I wouldn't sell him for a hundred. He may have taken a dislike to me, but I'll make him get over it.'

Heedless of Thunder's growling, he seized him by the collar and dragged him over to the car. As he tried to lift him in, the struggling dog clawed some paint off the mudguard. The city slicker lost his head and with his free hand beat him over the back. The dog continued to struggle, caught the hand that held his collar and bit it. The owner let go, and the dog went to lie against the presbytery wall, still growling. Don Camillo and Peppone stared from where they stood and did not have time to say a word. The city slicker, as pale as a corpse, pulled his shotgun out of the car and aimed it at the animal.

'You bastard!' he said between his teeth as he fired.

The wall of the rectory was stained with blood. After

a piercing howl, Thunder lay motionless on the ground. The city slicker got into his car and drove off at top speed. Don Camillo took no heed of his departure and did not notice that Peppone had followed on his motorcycle. He knelt beside the dog, with all his attention concentrated upon him. The dog groaned as Don Camillo stroked his head, and then suddenly licked his hand. Then he got up and barked happily.

After twenty minutes, Peppone returned. He was red in the face and his fists were clenched.

'I caught up with him at Fiumaccio, where he had to stop at the level crossing. I dragged him out of the car and boxed his ears until his head was as big as a watermelon. He reached for his gun, and I broke it over his back.'

They were in the hall, and now a howl came from farther inside.

'Isn't he dead yet?' asked Peppone.

'Only his flank was grazed,' said Don Camillo. 'In a week he'll be livelier than ever.'

Peppone ran a big hand doubtfully over his chin.

'Morally speaking,' said Don Camillo, 'he killed the dog. When he shot that was his intention. If Saint Anthony deflected his aim, that doesn't take away from the vileness of the deed. You were wrong to box his ears, because violence is never a good thing. But in any case ...'

'In any case ... he won't show his face here again,' said Peppone, 'and you have acquired a dog.'

'Half a dog,' declared Don Camillo. 'Because I'm morally indebted to you for the money you were ready to lend me. So half the dog is yours.'

Peppone scratched his head.

'Well, by all that's wonderful!' he exclaimed. 'An honest priest, and one that doesn't defraud the people!'

Don Camillo gave him a threatening look.

'Listen, if you bring politics into it, I'll change my mind and keep the dog to myself!'

'Consider it unsaid!' exclaimed Peppone, who underneath it all was a man and a hunter and cared more for Thunder's esteem than for that of Marx, Lenin, and company. And Thunder, with a bandage around his hips, came barking in to seal the pact of non-aggression.

21 · OPERATION SAINT BABILA

SAINT BABILA was perpetually in Don Camillo's way, but Don Camillo didn't know how in the world to get rid of him. On that far-away day when he first came to take over the parish he found Saint Babila in the sacristy, and there he left him. Every now and then he moved him from one corner to another, but Saint Babila continued to be cumbersome, because he was in the form of a lifesize terracotta statue, six feet tall and heavy as lead.

In the beginning the statue must have been properly robed and vested, with artistically painted face and hands, but the passage of time had caused all the ornamentation to fall to pieces, leaving the terracotta crude and bare. If it hadn't been for the worn inscription 'Saint Babila, B –' (for Bishop) on the base, no one would have thought there was anything holy about it. Several generations of acolytes had chosen to use it as a coat-rack, and as a result the head and shoulders looked as if they had been thoroughly sandpapered. From the waist, down it might have been modelled with a shovel, and from the waist up brushed with a chicken feather.

For years, then, Saint Babila had been a nuisance to Don Camillo. Any number of times he had thought of getting rid of him, but even though it is made of identical material, a saint's statue is not the same thing as a chipped kitchen pot. You can't take a hammer and smash it, or simply toss it into the dustbin. And even if banished to the cellar or woodshed it remains just as cumbersome as before. Don Camillo had in mind at one point to haul it all the way to the barn, but he was afraid that the loft floor would collapse under its weight. If only it had been made out of bronze, he could have melted it down and recast it as a bell. But how can a sacred image, sculptured in terracotta, be destroyed without profanity? One day, however, Don Camillo did find the answer, and he hurried at once to the sacristy to talk it over with Saint Babila.

The saint stood in one corner, his worn head and shoulders emerging from a crude vestment whose folds, moulded by some rustic potter, made it look as if it were a piece of corrugated sheet-iron.

'I have it!' said Don Camillo. 'And it's for your good as well as mine.' Then, removing the incense-pot censer which an irreverent acolyte had hung round the saint's neck, he continued:

'This is no place for you. Here there's no telling who may lay dirty hands upon you and fail to show the respect that is your due. I'm going to take you to a refuge where no one can touch you and you can abide in safety for ever and for ever. No, I'm not going to bury you underground, either. Underground means death, and running water is life-giving ...'

Don Camillo fancied he detected a grimace on the saint's worn face, and he protested impatiently:

'What about the "Christ of the Deep Sea" near Portofino? Wasn't his statue purposely lowered into the ocean bottom? You've no reason to make trouble! ...'

Saint Babila made no trouble, and that very night Don Camillo proceeded to carry out his plan. It required an immense physical effort, because the statue weighed over three hundred pounds. Finally, however, without being seen by a single soul, he succeeded in removing it from the sacristy and loading it on to a wagon. A few minutes later, with his overcoat pulled up to his hat-brim, he got into the driver's seat and drove towards the river. The night seemed particularly propitious to an Operation Saint Babila. It was freezing cold and the countryside was deserted.

When they reached the river, Don Camillo persuaded the horse to go all the way down to the water's edge, where with the help of two long boards he pushed the statue on to a rowing-boat. Then, having loosened the rope by which the boat was tied up, he took the oar and rowed towards midstream. He had a very clear idea of where he was going. The river, at this point, was so wide that it seemed like the sea and had a particularly deep bottom. This was to be the resting-place of Saint Babila.

At the last minute the saint abandoned his docile behaviour and made so much trouble that Don Camillo nearly fell overboard. But eventually the statue resigned itself to making the plunge and disappeared into the river.

When he got back home Don Camillo put the horse

in the stable and before going to bed went to pay his respects to the Christ over the main altar.

'Lord,' he said, 'thank you for not letting Saint Babila drag me into the water. I have reason to be happy tonight, because Saint Babila is settled *per omnia saecula saeculorum*, and that means for ever and ever.'

'*Amen*,' murmured Christ with a smile. 'But remember, Don Camillo, that in human events there are no absolutes.'

Operation Saint Babila had taken place between eleven-thirty and one-forty-five of a freezing November night, without a single soul to see. Don Camillo had conducted it with extreme prudence and had no cause for worry. But since in human events there are no absolutes, it happened that at one-forty-seven of the same night Comrade Peppone, the Communist mayor of the village, was awakened by a pole knocking against the shutters of his bedroom window. He got up and cautiously opened the shutters, to find that one of has Party henchmen, Smilzo, was standing below, at the far end of the pole, trembling with cold and excitement.

'Chief,' he shouted, 'something very serious has happened.'

Peppone went downstairs to open the door. As soon as Smilzo was in the house he exclaimed:

'A sacrilege!'

'A sacrilege?' echoed Peppone. 'Who's guilty of a sacrilege?'

'The priest!' shouted Smilzo.

Peppone took hold of Smilzo's ragged jacket and shook him violently.

'Smilzo, you must have been drinking.'

'Not I, Chief. The priest has committed a sacrilege, I tell you. I saw him with my own eyes and followed him the whole way. Do you remember the dusty statue of Saint Babila that stood in one corner of the sacristy?'

Peppone did remember. 'Saint Babila, B –' (for Blessed Virgin, he imagined), he must have read those words a thousand times on the base of the statue, which had most often been seen serving as a rack for coats and vestments.

'Well, I saw that statue, I tell you. He put it on a wagon and took it down to the river, then he transferred it to a boat and threw it into the water. I didn't see him actually throw it but I heard the splash, and when the boat came back there was no more no statue. That's a sacrilege, Chief!'

This was quite obviously true. Otherwise Don Camillo would not have feared the light of day. If he had done it all alone, in the dead of night, then there must have been something reprehensible about it.

This was the period of 'peaceful co-existence', when the Reds changed their line and passed themselves off as quiet folk, with a genuine respect for other people and especially for other people's religion. Peppone wasted no time. He got dressed and went with Smilzo to check up on what had taken place. Peeping through the sacristy window he saw that the statue had disappeared. Then he found the imprint of the horseshoes and the track left by the wagon-wheels, all leading down to the river. On the shore there was a still more important piece of evidence. While Don Camillo was transferring the statue to the boat, a fragment had been chipped off and now lay there, bearing witness to the truth of Smilzo's story. With all these elements in hand, Peppone sent Smilzo to gather his henchmen together. At eleven o'clock the next morning the village was plastered with posters carrying the following message:

Citizens:

Under cover of darkness a sacrilegious hand profaned

the Lord's House and stole the sacred image of the Virgin Saint Babila. In order to abolish its veneration and to uproot even its memory from the hearts of the faithful, this same sacred image was then, most nefariously, thrown into the river.

Before this ignoble deed the local section of the Communist Party cannot but lay aside its political enmity towards the clerical intriguers. Along with all good Christians we deplore this loss and intend to organize a searching party, whose mission is to restore Saint Babila to the place of honour which she held before.

Giuseppe Bottazzi

Everyone that read these words hastened to the church, and since the whole village read them the church was soon overcrowded and Don Camillo was in serious trouble. People wanted to know how, when, and why, and he couldn't very well answer: 'There was no theft and no sacrilege. I am the one that threw the statue into the river.' Suddenly now that the statue was gone, all the villagers, including those who were completely unaware of its existence, declared that it was the church's most treasured possession. Words could not express the resentment they harboured against the thief.

When Don Camillo could stand no more, he threw out his arms in a gesture of despair and fled to the rectory, where he took to his bed with a raging fever.

'Poor Don Camillo!' said his parishioners. 'He's overcome by sorrow.'

Meanwhile the proponents of the 'peaceful co-existence' line had gone into action, and the next morning they were hot on the trail, down by the river. From a motor-boat, where he cut the figure of an admiral, Peppone directed dredging operations. In the area pointed out by Smilzo not a single inch of the river bottom was left untouched. And when the workers came back to the shore for lunch, Peppone announced:

'If we're unsuccessful we'll call upon the union of deep-sea divers. Saint Babila shall be found; we have sworn it before God and the people!'

This fine phrase made the round of the entire village. Meanwhile, after lunch, the dredging was resumed, and soon the search centred about the deepest part of the river. All of a sudden a cry passed from mouth to mouth on the shore:

'They're getting hot!'

And half an hour later there was a loud explosion of joy:

'Saint Babila is found!'

Don Camillo was still nursing his fever and trying to keep his mind off his troubles when they were quite forcibly called to his attention. A crowd of excited men and women burst into his room shouting:

'Father, they've fished up the statue!'

'Father, they're forming a procession on the bank of the river!'

'Father, the procession is on its way, bringing the statue home!'

'The whole village is marching, and a lot more people from the country around!'

'Father, you'll simply have to get up and receive them!'

The procession was indeed drawing near. When Don Camillo sat up in bed and looked out of the window he could see a multitude of people winding their way along and singing: 'Look down on the people, Thou Blessed One', to the music of the local brass band. There was nothing to do but get dressed and go downstairs. He threw open the church door and stood there, waiting for Saint Babila.

They had put the statue on a litter, borne on the shoulders of the eight liveliest devils of Peppone's gang, with Peppone himself and his closest cronies preceding it. Behind the litter came the brass band, followed by some two or three thousand people. Those of the villagers who had stayed at home scattered flowers from their windows.

When the head of the procession reached the church square and the litter-bearers were in front of the door, Peppone signalled to them to lay their burden gently down. The winding line broke up and rushed forward. When the crowd had gathered round him Peppone turned to Don Camillo and said in a thundering voice:

'Father, the people's callous but honest hands have brought you back the venerable image of their protectress, Saint Babila, stolen by some sacrilegious criminal but washed and purified in the waters of our country's mightiest river!'

Don Camillo wished for his eyes to be transformed into loaded machine-guns, but all he could do was bow his head as if to say: 'Thank you, Mr Mayor. May the heavens open and strike you dead!'

After this a group of true believers took the place of Peppone's henchmen and Saint Babila was carried triumphantly into the church. Naturally the statue could not be banished to the sacristy. The image of Saint Lucius, patron of dairy-farmers, was moved out of one of the chapels in order to give it an honoured place.

An hour later, when peace and quiet were restored, the wife of Bigio came to the church to have her latest offspring baptized. The baby was a girl, and if she hadn't been the offspring of a rascally infidel, she might have been called pretty.

'What do you want to call her?' asked Don Camillo between clenched teeth.

'Babila,' the mother answered defiantly.

'That won't do,' said Don Camillo.

'And why not?' said the mother with a sarcastic laugh. 'Just because our Party fished the saint out of the river?'

'No,' said Don Camillo glumly. 'Because Babila is a man's name.'

The woman shook her head and turned to look at the saint. On the base was printed: 'Saint Babila, B –'

'Saint Babila, Blessed, I suppose,' she said, laughing again.

'No,' said Don Camillo, 'that *B* is for "Bishop".'

The mother, the godparents, and their friends looked at one another disappointedly.

'A bishop!' the mother muttered ill-humouredly. 'We might as well have left him at the bottom of the river!'

'Very well, then,' said Don Camillo, grinding his teeth; 'what's to be the name?'

The little group wore a puzzled air.

'Palmira, like our leader, Palmiro Togliatti,' one suggested.

'Marilyn,' said the godmother, who was a passionate reader of film magazines.

And Marilyn it was.

22 · THE NEW LOOK

When the official news came through, along with the first directives, Peppone was staggered. In the good old days he had fought like a lion to have one of the village streets called after Joseph Stalin and had even given his name to the Consumer's Co-operative. As if this were not enough, the great hall of his emporium and meeting-place was decorated with a bigger-than-life-size portrait of the great man.

Such was Peppone's discomfiture that when he had called his henchmen together he found himself for the first time with nothing to say. All he did was toss the sheet of paper containing the directives on to the table and throw out his arms in a helpless and disconsolate manner. The others read the paper through and looked at one another. Then Smilzo summed up the situation.

'What fault have we, Chief, if we believed what the higher-ups told us? Anyhow, it's all perfectly simple. We take down the street sign, change the Co-operative's name, and splash a bucket of whitewash over that wall. Stalinism has gone down the drain.'

They had met in the Co-operative, and on the wall in front of them was the gigantic portrait of the moustachioed, posthumously purged Leader. Peppone looked at it very sadly. He suffered not only from the blow to his faith, but from a vivid memory of the amount of money the portrait had cost. He himself had insisted that it be a fresco, because, as he had declared at the unveiling, 'it must endure as long as the glory of the father of all peoples, that is, for ever and ever'.

In the great hall were gathered only Peppone and his general staff; the hoi polloi were playing cards and listening to the radio in two other rooms. Thus they were spared the sight of the discredited leader, while Peppone and his intimates could discuss the situation more freely. Naturally enough, when Don Camillo's voice suddenly boomed forth in their midst they started as if a cannon had sounded.

'Good evening,' he said heartily, and went to sit down at a small table.

'This hall is reserved for private deliberations,' Smilzo told him.

Don Camillo settled back in his chair, stuck a cigar butt between his lips, and calmly lit it.

'Is there some celebration?' he asked, after he had blown a smoke-ring up at the ceiling.

'When a visitor sees that he's not wanted,' put in Peppone, 'the least he can do is go away without stopping to argue.'

'Certainly,' said Don Camillo. 'But when a visitor is taking advantage of his last chance to admire a masterpiece of art which is about to be destroyed, then, wanted or not wanted, it's his duty to remain.'

He scrutinized the painting on the wall with a connoisseur's eye and then ended:

'Because it's a fresco, you'll have to scrape and replaster the wall. Twelve square yards of plastering are no joke.'

There was no reply. Peppone clenched his fists but held his tongue.

'Oh well, politics is politics. I don't run the same risk, thank heaven. My Leader's held his own for nearly two thousand years.'

Peppone jumped to his feet.

'Father,' he said, 'if you want to pick a fight, you've come to the right place.'

Don Camillo shook his head.

'Never again, Mr Mayor, never again! We've fought quite often enough over that fellow with the bushy moustache. I came simply to indulge in the legitimate satisfaction of seeing you destroy the image of your former god.'

Peppone brought his fist down on the table and shouted:

'You shan't have that satisfaction!'

Again Don Camillo shook his head.

'Mr Mayor, you've misunderstood me. I don't say that you must take a hammer and start to knock off the plaster in my sight. I just want to know that you've given orders for the demolition. Farewell, Face! ...'

Peppone brought down his other fist on the table.

'I'm giving no such orders. As long as I live, that face won't be touched.'

'Then you're disobeying the higher-ups. You're running foul of Party discipline.'

'No, I'm not,' shouted Peppone. 'The Party doesn't

order me to give satisfaction to a rascally priest or other such garbage.'

When Don Camillo had left home it wasn't with the intention of getting Peppone into so much trouble, but now that things had taken this turn he let him stew in his own juice.

'Well, do as you see fit,' he retorted blandly. 'But at least I'll have the satisfaction of seeing Stalin's name obliterated from the façade of the Co-operative and the street sign.'

'You shan't see anything at all!' shouted Peppone.

Peppone got into really hot water because the reactionary papers took up the story and carried pieces about 'deviations', 'Stalinist factions', and 'possible splits'. Very soon a bright young man was sent from national headquarters. He called a meeting of Peppone's chief henchmen and addressed them as follows:

'The reactionary papers are printing the usual absurd stories, but there's no use contradicting them. The only answer is to go ahead and get rid of the painting and the street sign and the name on the façade of the building, as originally intended.'

The man from headquarters was a stickler for discipline, the sort of young Party worker that wears spectacles and a double-breasted suit. But he made no impression on Peppone.

'My personal prestige is at stake,' Peppone told him. 'We're not getting rid of anything. I won't hear of giving that miserable priest such satisfaction.'

The man from headquarters tried to explain that where the dignity of the Party is involved, that of the individual must take second place. He brought in the dangers of the 'personality cult' and its terrible consequences. Then, when he saw that Peppone was still looking askance at him, he thought up a compromise solution.

'Comrade, I know how to reconcile our points of

view. We'll send you off on a mission, and while you're away, your men will obey our orders to wipe everything out.'

Bigio was a man of few words, and those he did speak tumbled out of his mouth like bricks falling from the top of a scaffolding.

'It will have to be *your* men that carry out *your* orders. We're not wiping out a thing. You got us into all this trouble. Why couldn't you tell us before he died just how things stood?'

The man from headquarters looked round and then explained that he was only a link in the chain of command.

'Very well, then,' he concluded. 'I'll make a report on your objections.'

He did exactly this, and as a result Peppone received an ultimatum; either to knuckle under or else to be expelled from the Party for indiscipline and other damaging reasons.

It was a peremptory letter, and having read it several times Peppone went to the rectory and threw it down in front of Don Camillo. Don Camillo read it over and over in his turn and then came out with the single word:

'Garibaldi.'

'Garibaldi?' muttered Peppone suspiciously. 'Where does he come in?'

'Because he has the same first name as Stalin, and you can leave the first half of the inscription on the façade of the Co-operative the way it is. As for the painting, you don't need to deface it. You can just pierce a hole and put in a glass door connecting the great hall with the pergola and the bowling-alley. As for the street sign, never mind about that. One day it will fall, all by itself.'

Peppone pounded his fists on the table and thrust his chin out in the direction of Don Camillo.

'I said I wasn't going to give you any satisfaction!'

'I don't want any. You've won, and this is my surrender. You're the stronger of the two.'

'Father, I can't trust you. There's something here that doesn't meet the eye.'

'Only a little common sense,' said Don Camillo, shaking his head. 'I'd rather have a live Peppone than a dead Stalin. It's better to thumb a nose at Stalin than at you. Just think it over and see if you don't agree.'

Peppone thought for a moment, and then said:

'From my point of view, you're quite right.'

'From mine too ... Lambrusco wine or Fontanella?'

'Lambrusco,' said Peppone without hesitation.

It was an unusually fine bottle and so were the two that followed. At a certain point Peppone raised his glass and shouted:

'Hurrah for Garibaldi!'

'Hurrah!' said Don Camillo, clinking his glass against the other.

Then they had to drink a toast to the conscripts born in 1899, iron men, one and all.

'We ninety-niners! ...' exclaimed Peppone.

And he said these three words in such a way that they were as meaningful as a long oration.

23 · BENEFIT OF CLERGY

THE time had come to speak of Smilzo, official messenger at the Town Hall and head of the 'flying squad' of the local Communist Party, and to brand him for what he was, an example of flagrant immorality, a man without any sense of shame, because a man must be shameless to live openly with a woman to whom he is not married in the village of the Po valley. And the woman who shared his bed and board was just as shameless as he.

People called Moretta a 'kept woman', but in reality she was a girl quite capable of keeping herself. She was big-boned and as strong as any man, and farmers hired her to run a tractor, which she manoeuvred just as skilfully as Peppone. Although the women of the village referred to her as 'that hussy', no man but Smilzo had ever made advances to her without getting a slap in the face that left him groggy. Nevertheless, it was a village scandal to see him carry her on the handlebars of his bicycle, which was where she rode when she didn't occupy the saddle and carry him.

Don Camillo had come into the world with a constitutional preference for calling a spade a spade and so it was that he spoke from the pulpit of 'certain women who rode around on racing bicycles, flaunting their flanks as freely as their faces'. From then on, Moretta wore blue dungarees and a red kerchief around her neck, which left the village even more shocked than before. Once Don Camillo managed to catch hold of Smilzo and say something to him about 'legalizing the situation', but Smilzo only jeered in his face.

'There's nothing to "legalize" about it. We do nothing more and nothing less than people who are idiotic enough to get married.'

'Than decent men and women ...' Don Camillo sputtered.

'Than idiots who spoil the beauty of affinity between two united souls by dragging a clumsy oaf of a mayor or a priest reeking of tobacco into it.'

Don Camillo swallowed the aspersion on his tobacco and came back to the main point of what he was saying. But Smilzo continued to jeer at him.

'If God Almighty had intended men and women to be joined in matrimony, He'd have put a priest with Adam and Eve in the Garden of Eden! Love was born free and free it ought to remain! The day is coming when people will understand that marriage is like a jail sentence, and they'll get along without benefit of clergy. And when that day comes there'll be dancing in the churches.'

Don Camillo found only a brick handy. He picked this up and threw it, but Smilzo had learned during the period of the Resistance movement to slip between one volley of machine-gun fire and another, and so the brick was wasted. But Don Camillo was not discouraged, and one day he lured Moretta to the presbytery. She came in her blue dungarees, with the red kerchief around her neck, and lit a cigarette as soon as she sat down before him. Don Camillo refrained from scolding her and spoke in the mildest tone of voice he could manage.

'You're a hard-working girl and a good housekeeper,' he told her. 'I know that you don't gossip or waste money. And I know too that you love your husband...'

'He isn't my husband,' Moretta interrupted.

'That you love Smilzo, then,' said Don Camillo patiently. 'And so, although you've never come to confession, I'm convinced that you're a decent sort of woman. Why do you have to behave in such a way that people brand you as indecent?'

' "People" can go straight to ... where they belong,' Moretta retorted.

Don Camillo was growing red in the face, but he went ahead with his plan and murmured something about getting married. But Moretta interrupted him.

'If God Almighty had intended men and women to be joined in matrimony ...'

'Never mind,' said Don Camillo, interrupting her in his turn. 'I know the rest already.'

'Love was born free and free it ought to remain!' Moretta concluded gravely. 'Marriage is the opium of love.'

The village gossips did not give up so easily. They

formed a committee and went to tell the Mayor that the affair was bringing shame upon the village and for the sake of public morals he must do something about it.

'I'm married myself,' said Peppone, 'and I have a right to perform a civil marriage, but I can't force people to marry when they don't want to. That's the law. Perhaps when the Pope comes into power things will be different.'

But the old crones insisted.

'If you can't do anything as Mayor, then as head of the local section of the Party you can bring pressure on them. They're a disgrace to the Party, too.'

'I'll try,' said Peppone, and so he did.

'I'd rather join the *Socialist* Party than marry,' was Smilzo's answer.

That was all there was to it, and with the passage of time the scandal abated, or rather politics took its place. But one day it came to the fore again and in a clamorous manner. For some time Comrade Moretta was not seen about, and then all of a sudden there was a startling piece of news. There were no longer two Comrades, but three, because, as the midwife told it, a little girl had been born to them, and one far prettier than they deserved. The old crones of the village began to wag their tongues again, and those who were politically-minded said:

'There are Communist morals for you. It's a hundred to one these godless parents will never have the child baptized.'

The news and the comment reached Peppone's ears, and he rushed to the godless parents' home.

Don Camillo was reading when Smilzo came in.

'There's a baptizing job for you to do,' Smilzo said abruptly.

'A fine job indeed,' muttered Don Camillo.

'Must one obtain a *nihil obstat* before having a baby?' Smilzo asked him.

'The *nihil obstat* of your own conscience,' said Don Camillo. 'But that's strictly your affair. Only if Moretta arrives dressed in her blue dungarees, I'll chase you all away. You can come twenty minutes from now.'

Moretta came with the baby in her arms and Smilzo at her side. Don Camillo received them along with Peppone and his wife at the door to the church.

'Take all that red stuff off,' he said, without even looking to see if they really were wearing anything red. 'This is the House of God and not the People's Palace.'

'There's nothing red around here except the fog in your brain,' muttered Peppone.

They went into the church and over to the baptismal font, where Don Camillo began the ceremony.

'What's the name?' he asked.

'Rita Palmira Valeria,' the mother stated firmly.

There was a dead silence as the three names – every one of them of internationally famous Communists – echoed in the little church. Don Camillo replaced the cover on the font and was just about to say 'then go and get her baptized in Russia' when he saw the Lord looking down at him from the Cross. So he just took a deep breath and counted to ten instead.

'Rita is for my mother, Palmira for his, and Valeria for my grandmother,' Moretta pointed out.

'That's their bad luck,' said Don Camillo dryly. 'I say Emilia Rosa Antonietta.'

Peppone pawed the ground, while Smilzo sighed and shook his head, but Moretta seemed secretly pleased.

Afterwards they went to the presbytery to sign the register.

'Under the Christian Democrat Government, is Palmira a forbidden name?' Peppone asked sarcastically.

Don Camillo did not answer, but motioned to him

and his wife to go home. Smilzo, Moretta, and the baby were left standing in front of the table.

'Enciclica rerarum novium,' said Smilzo more cleverly than correctly, with the look of a man resigned to his fate.

'No. I'm not making a speech,' Don Camillo said coldly. 'I just want to give you a warning. By not getting married you are not hurting the Church. You're just two cockroaches trying to gnaw at one of the columns of Saint Peter's. Neither you nor your offspring are of the slightest interest to me.'

At this moment the bundle in Moretta's arms stirred, and the 'offspring' opened her eyes wide and smiled at Don Camillo. She had such a pink little face that Don Camillo paused and then his blood began to boil and he lost his temper.

'Miserable creatures!' he shouted. 'You have no right to visit your foolish sins upon the head of this innocent baby. She's going to grow up to be a beautiful girl and when people are envious of her beauty they'll throw mud at her by calling her a "kept woman's child". If you weren't such wretches you wouldn't expose your daughter to people's jealous hypocrisy. You may not care what people say about you, but if on your account they slander her ...'

Don Camillo had raised his fist and thrown out his chest so that he looked even taller and bigger than he was, and the two parents had taken refuge in a corner.

'Get married, you criminals!' the priest shouted.

Pale and perspiring, Smilzo shook his head.

'No; that would be the end of everything for us. We couldn't face people.'

The baby seemed to enjoy the scene. She waved her hands and laughed, and Don Camillo was taken aback.

'Please, I'm begging you!' he exclaimed. 'She's too beautiful!'

Strange things can happen in this world. A man may try with a crowbar to force a door open and not move it a single inch. Then when he is dead tired and hangs his hat on the knob in order to wipe the sweat off his brow, click, the door opens. Moretta was a stubborn woman, but when she saw that Don Camillo's anger was dying down as he looked at her baby, she threw herself on to a chair and began to cry.

'No, no,' she sobbed. 'We can't marry because we're married already. We did it three years ago, only nobody knows, because we chose somewhere far away. We've always liked free love. And so we've never told a soul.'

Smilzo nodded.

'Marriage is the opium of love,' he began. 'Love was born free, and if God Almighty . . .'

Don Camillo went to douse his face in cold water. When he came back, Smilzo and his wife were quite calm, and Moretta was holding out a paper which was a marriage certificate.

'Under the secrecy of the confessional,' she whispered.

Don Camillo nodded.

'So you've registered with your employer as "single",' he said to Smilzo, 'and you don't get any of the benefits of being a family man.'

'Exactly,' said Smilzo. 'There's nothing I wouldn't do for my ideals.'

Don Camillo handed back the certificate.

'You're two donkeys,' he said calmly. Then, when the baby smiled, he corrected himself: 'Two donkeys and a half.'

Smilzo turned round at the door and raised a clenched fist in salute.

'There'll always be a place on the gallows for those who run down the people,' he said gravely.

'You'd better hang your hat on it then, so as to

reserve a place for yourself!' answered Don Camillo.

'The election we lost was just a passing phase,' said Smilzo. 'We have come from very far and we still have far to go. Farewell, citizen priest.'

24 · HOLIDAY JOYS

IN retaliation for excommunication, the Reds decided to abolish Christmas.

And so on Christmas Eve Peppone came out of the People's Palace without so much as a glance at Bigio, who was waiting for him at the door, and hurried home, avoiding the main square in order not to run into the crowd returning from Midnight Mass. Smilzo trailed after him in disciplined style, but got no reward for his pains, because Peppone slammed the door of his own house behind him without so much as a goodnight. He was dead tired and lost no time in falling into bed.

'Is that you?' asked his wife.

'Yes,' mumbled Peppone. 'Who do you expect it to be?'

'There's no telling,' she retorted. 'With the new principles you've just announced, it might just as well be some other official of your Party.'

'Don't be silly,' said Peppone. 'I'm not in a joking mood.'

'Neither am I, after this very uninspiring Christmas Eve. You wouldn't even look at the letter your son had left under your plate. And when he stood up on a chair to recite the Christmas poem he learned in school you ran away. What have children to do with politics, anyhow?'

'Let me sleep, will you?' shouted Peppone, rolling over and over.

She stopped talking, but it took Peppone a long time to fall asleep. Even after he finally dozed off, he found no peace, for nightmares assailed him, the kind of nightmares that go with indigestion or worry. He woke up while it was still dark, jumped out of bed, and got dressed without putting on the light.

He went down to the kitchen to heat some milk and found the table set just the way it was the evening before. The soup bowl was still there and he lifted it up to look for the little boy's letter, but it was gone. He looked at the spotted tablecloth and the scraps of food upon it, remembering how his wife once decorated the table on past Christmas Eves. This led him to think of other Christmases, when he was a boy, and of his father and mother.

Suddenly he had a vivid memory of Christmas 1944, which he had spent in the mountains, crouching in a cave in danger of being machine-gunned from one moment to the next. That was a terrible Christmas, indeed, and yet it wasn't so bad as this one because he had thought all day of the good things that went with a peacetime celebration, and the mere thought had warmed the cockles of his heart.

Now there was no danger, and everything was going smoothly. His wife and children were there right in the next room, and he had only to open the door in order to hear their quiet breathing. But his heart was icy cold at the thought that the festive table would be just as melancholy on Christmas Day as it had been the evening before.

'And yet that's all there is to Christmas,' he said to himself. 'It's just a matter of shiny glasses, snow-white napkins, roast capons and rich desserts.'

Then he thought again of Lungo's little boy, who had built a clandestine Manger in the attic of the People's Palace. And of the letter and poem of his own little boy, which had no connection with all the foodstuffs he had insisted were only the true symbols of the season.

It was starting to grow light as Peppone walked in his long black cape from his own house to the People's Palace. Lungo was already up and busy sweeping the assembly room. Peppone was amazed to find him at the door.

'Are you at work this early?'

'It's seven o'clock,' Lungo explained. 'On ordinary days, I start at eight, but today isn't ordinary.'

Peppone went to his desk and started looking over the mail. There were only a dozen routine letters, and within a few minutes his job was done.

'Nothing important, Chief?' asked Lungo, sticking his head around the door.

'Nothing at all,' said Peppone. 'You can take care of them yourself.'

Lungo picked up the letters and went away, but he came back soon after with a sheet of paper in his hands.

'This is important, Chief,' he said. 'It must have escaped your notice.'

Peppone took the letter, looked at it and handed it back.

'Oh, I saw that,' he said; 'there's nothing unusual about it.'

'But it's a matter of Party membership and you really ought to make an immediate reply.'

'Some other day,' mumbled Peppone. 'This is Christmas.'

Lungo gave him a stare which Peppone didn't like. He got up and stood squarely in front of his subordinate.

'I said it's Christmas, did you understand?'

'No, I didn't,' said Lungo, shaking his head.

'Then I'll explain,' said Peppone, giving him a monumental slap in the face.

Lungo made the mistake of continuing to play dumb, and because he was a strapping fellow, even bigger than Peppone, he gave him back a dose of the same medicine. With which Peppone charged like an armoured division, knocked him on to the floor and proceeded to change the complexion of his hindquarters with a series of swift kicks. When he had done a thorough job, he grabbed Lungo by the lapels and asked him:

'Did you understand what I was saying?'

'I get it; today's Christmas,' said Lungo darkly.

Peppone stared at the little Manger Lungo's son had built.

'What does it matter if some people choose to believe that a carpenter's son, born two thousand years ago, went out to preach the equality of all men and to defend the poor against the rich, only to be crucified by the age-old enemies of justice and liberty?'

'That doesn't matter at all,' said Lungo, shaking his big head. 'The trouble is that some people insist he was the son of God. That's the ugly part of it.'

'Ugly?' exclaimed Peppone. 'I think it's beautiful, if you want to know. The fact that God chose a carpenter and not a rich man for a father shows that He is deeply democratic.'

Lungo sighed. 'Too bad the priests are mixed up in it,' he said. 'Otherwise we could take it over.'

'Exactly! Now you've hit the real point. We must keep our heads and not mix up things that have no real connection. God is one thing and priests are another. And the danger comes not from God but from the priests. They're what we must seek to eliminate. It's the same thing with rich people's money. We must eliminate them and distribute their money among the poor.'

Lungo's political education had not gone so far, and once more he shook his head uncomprehendingly.

'That isn't the essential question. The fact is that God doesn't exist; he's merely a priests' invention. The only things that really exist are those that we can see and touch for ourselves. All the rest is sheer fancy.'

Peppone didn't seem to put much stock in Lungo's cerebrations, for he answered:

'If a man's born blind, how is he to know that red, green, and the other colours exist, since he can't see them? Suppose all of us were to be born blind; then within a hundred years all belief in the existence of colour would be lost. And yet you and I can vouch for it. Isn't it possible that God exists and we are blind men who on the basis of reason or experience alone can't understand His existence?'

Lungo was completely baffled.

'Never mind,' said Peppone abruptly. 'This isn't a problem that requires immediate solution. Forget about it.'

Peppone was on his way home when he ran into Don Camillo.

'What can I do for Your Grey Eminence?' he asked gloomily.

'I wanted to offer you my best wishes for Christmas and the New Year,' said Don Camillo blandly.

'You forget that we Reds have been excommunicated,' said Peppone. 'That makes your good wishes somewhat illogical.'

'No more illogical that the care which a doctor gives a sick man. He may quarantine him in order to protect others from his contagious disease, but he continues to look after him. We abhor not the sinner but his sin.'

'That's a good one!' said Peppone. 'You talk of love, but you'd kill us off without hesitation.'

'No, we'd be very poor doctors of men's souls if we killed them in order to obtain a cure. Our love is directed at their healing.'

'And what about the violent cure you spoke of at the political rally the other day?'

'That had nothing to do with you and your friends,' Don Camillo answered calmly. 'Take typhus for instance. There are three elements involved. The typhus itself, the lice that carry it and the suffering patient. In order to overcome the disease we must care for the patient and kill the lice. It would be idiotic to care for the lice and insane to imagine that they could be transformed into something other than a vehicle of contagion. And in this case, Peppone, you are the sick man, not the louse.'

'I'm perfectly well, thank you, Father. You're the sick one, sick in the head.'

'Anyhow, my Christmas wishes come not from the head but from the heart; you can accept them without reservation.'

'No,' said Peppone, 'head, heart, or liver, it's all the same. That's like saying: "Here's a nice little bullet for you; it's a gift not from the percussion cap but from the barrel."'

Don Camillo threw out his arms in discouragement.

'God will take pity on you,' he murmured.

'That may be, but I doubt that He'll take pity on you. Come the revolution, He won't prevent your hanging from that pole. Do you see it?'

Of course Don Camillo saw the flagpole. The People's Palace was on the right side of the square and from his study window he couldn't help seeing the pole sticking insolently up into the free air, with a shiny metal hammer and sickle at its summit. This was quite enough to ruin the view.

'Don't you think I may be a bit too heavy for your pole?' he asked Peppone. 'Hadn't you better import some gallows from Prague? Or are those reserved for Party comrades?'

Peppone turned his back and went away. When he reached his own house he called his wife outside.

'I'll be back about one o'clock,' he told her. 'Try to fix everything in the usual Christmas way.'

'That's already attended to,' she mumbled. 'You'd better be back by noon.'

Shortly after noon, when he came into the big kitchen, Peppone rediscovered the atmosphere of Christmases gone by and felt as if he were emerging from a nightmare. The little boy's Christmas letter was under his plate and seemed to him unusually well written. He was ready and eager to hear the Christmas poem, but this did not seem to be forthcoming. He imagined it would come at the end of the meal and went on eating. Even when they had finished dinner, however, the child showed no intention of standing up in his chair to recite, in the customary manner. Peppone looked questioningly at his wife, but she only shrugged her shoulders in reply. She whispered something in the little boy's ear and then reported to her husband:

'Nothing doing. He won't say it.'

Peppone had a secret weapon; a box of chocolates

which he extracted from his pocket with the announcement:

'If someone recites a poem, this is his reward!'

The child looked anxiously at the chocolates but continued to shake his head. His mother parleyed with him again but brought back the same negative reply. At this point Peppone lost patience.

'If you won't recite the poem, it means you don't know it!' he said angrily.

'I know it, all right,' the child answered, 'but it can't be recited now.'

'Why not?' Peppone shouted.

'Because it's too late. The Baby Jesus is born now, and the poem is about the time just before.'

Peppone called for the notebook and found that, sure enough, the poem was all in the future tense. At midnight the stall at Bethlehem would be lit up, the Infant would be born and the shepherds would come to greet Him.

'But a poem's not like an advertisement in the paper,' said Peppone. 'Even if it's a day old it's just as good as it was to start with.'

'No,' the child insisted, 'if Baby Jesus was born last night, we can't talk about him as going to be born tomorrow.'

His mother urged him again, but he would not give in.

In the afternoon Peppone took the little boy for a walk and when they were far from home he made one more attempt to bring him around.

'Now that we're all alone, can't you recite the poem?'

'No.'

'No one will hear you.'

'But Baby Jesus will know.'

This sentence was a poem itself, and Peppone appreciated it.

*

The allotted number of days went by and then New Year's Eve arrived in the village. In the little world as everywhere else it was the custom to welcome the New Year with lots of noise. The irrepressible high spirits of the villagers found this an excellent excuse for letting go with every available firearm at midnight. So the New Year was started off right and the dying year killed off for good and all. Don Camillo had a hundred good reasons for disliking this custom, but this year he felt a perverse desire to kill the old year and have done with it. A few minutes before midnight he opened his study window and stood there, gun in hand, waiting for the bell in the church tower to ring. The lights were out but there was a fire in the fireplace and when Thunder, his dog, caught the gleam of the gun in Don Camillo's hand he was highly excited.

'Quiet there,' Don Camillo explained. 'This isn't my shooting gun. It's the old firing-piece I keep in the attic. It's a matter of shooting the old year out, and a shotgun won't answer the purpose.'

The square was empty and the lamp in front of the People's Palace lit up the flagpole.

'It's almost as conspicuous by night as it is by day,' muttered Don Camillo. 'Seems as if they put it there just to annoy me.'

The first of the twelve peals of midnight sounded, and at once the shooting began. Don Camillo leaned on the window-sill calmly and fired a single shot. Just one, because the gesture was a symbolic one and this was quite sufficient to give it meaning. It was very cold. Don Camillo carefully shut the window, leaned the gun against a chest and stirred the fire. All of a sudden he realized that Thunder wasn't there. Obviously he was so excited over the shooting that he had run out to join the fun. The priest was not particularly worried. The dog would slip back in just as easily as he had slipped out a few minutes before. Soon after this the door creaked and he looked up expectantly. The cause was not Thunder but Peppone.

'Excuse me,' he said, 'but the door was ajar and I came to pay you a call.'

'Thank you, my son. It's always pleasant to be remembered.'

'Father,' said Peppone, sitting down beside him. 'There's no doubt about it: truth is stranger than fiction.'

'Has something unfortunate happened?' asked Don Camillo.

'No, just a curious coincidence. Someone shooting into the air hit our flagpole just at the top, where the metal emblem is joined on to the wood. Don't you find that extraordinary?'

'Extraordinary indeed,' Don Camillo agreed, throwing out his arms.

'And that's not all,' Peppone continued. 'In its fall the emblem very nearly hit Lungo on the head. He thought someone had thrown something at him on purpose and gave the alarm. We all went out to look, and although there was nothing on the ground we noticed when we looked up that the emblem was missing from the flagpole and that, as I told you, it had been clipped off very neatly. Now who do you think can have taken it away as a trophy from the deserted square?'

'To be quite frank,' said Don Camillo, 'I can't imagine who would be interested in a piece of junk of that kind.'

Meanwhile Thunder had come back in and sat motionless between the two men. The hammer-and-sickle emblem was between his teeth and at a certain point he dropped it on to the floor. Don Camillo picked it up and turned it around in his hand.

'A poor quality of metal,' he said. 'From a distance it didn't look so frail. Take it home if it interests you.'

Peppone looked at the emblem which Don Camillo was holding out to him and then looked into the fire. Since no hand was extended to take it, the priest threw it into the flames. Peppone gritted his teeth but said nothing. The emblem grew red hot, its joints melted and the various parts curled up like so many snakes.

'If Hell weren't just an invention of us priests ...' Don Camillo murmured.

'It's the other way around,' muttered Peppone. 'Priests are an invention of Hell!'

While the priest poked at the fire Peppone went to look out the window. Through the glass he could see the decapitated flagpole.

'How many shots did it take you?' he asked without turning around.

'One.'

'American model with telescope attachment?'

'No, a regular old ninety-one.'

Peppone came to sit down again by the fire.

'That's still a good gun,' he mumbled.

'Guns are ugly things at best,' murmured Don Camillo.

'Happy New Year!' muttered Peppone as he went out the door.

'Thanks, and the same to you,' Don Camillo answered.

'I was speaking to Thunder,' said Peppone roughly.

And Thunder, who was stretched out in front of the fire, responded to the mention of his name by wagging his tail.

25 · TECHNIQUE OF THE *COUP D'ÉTAT*

AT ten o'clock on Tuesday evening the village square was swept with wind and rain, but a crowd had been gathered there for three or four hours to listen to the election news coming out of a radio loudspeaker. Suddenly the lights went out and everything was plunged into darkness. Someone went to the control box but came back saying there was nothing to be done. The trouble must be up the line or at the power plant, miles away. People hung around for a half-hour or so, and then, as the rain began to come down even harder than before, they scattered to their homes, leaving the village silent and deserted. Peppone shut himself up in the People's Palace, along with Lungo, Brusco, Straziami, and Gigio, the lame leader of the 'Red Wing' squad from Molinetto. They sat around uneasily by the light of a candle stump and cursed the power and light monopoly as an enemy of the people, until Smilzo burst in. He had gone to Roccaverde on his motor-cycle to see if anyone had news, and now his eyes were popping out of his head and he was waving a sheet of paper.

'The Front has won!' he panted. 'Fifty-two seats out of a hundred in the Senate and fifty-one in the Chamber. The other side is done for. We must get hold of our people and have a celebration. If there's no light, we can set fire to a couple of haystacks nearby.'

'Hurrah!' shouted Peppone. But Gigio grabbed hold of Smilzo's jacket.

'Keep quiet and stay where you are!' he said grimly. 'It's too early for anyone to be told. Let's take care of our little list.'

'List? What list?' asked Peppone in astonishment.

'The list of reactionaries who are to be executed first thing. Let's see now ...'

Peppone stammered that he had made no such list, but the other only laughed.

'That doesn't matter. I've a very complete one here all ready. Let's look at it together, and once we've decided, we can get to work.'

Gigio pulled a sheet of paper with some twenty names on it out of his pocket and laid it on the table.

'Looks to me as if all the reactionary pigs are here,' he said. 'I put down the worst of them, and we can attend to the rest later.'

Peppone scanned the names and scratched his head.

'Well, what do you say?' Gigio asked him.

'Generally speaking, we agree,' said Peppone. 'But what's the hurry? We have plenty of time to do things in the proper style.'

Gigio brought his fist down on the table.

'We haven't a minute to lose, that's what I say,' he shouted harshly. 'This is the time to put our hands on them, before they suspect us. If we wait until tomorrow, they may get wind of something and disappear.'

At this point Brusco came into the discussion.

'You must be crazy,' he said. 'You can't start out to kill people before you think it over.'

'I'm not crazy, and you're a very poor Communist, that's what you are! These are all reactionary pigs; no one can dispute that, and if you don't take advantage of this golden opportunity then you're a traitor to the Party!'

Brusco shook his head.

'Don't you believe it! It's jackasses that are traitors to the Party! And you'll be a jackass if you make mistakes and slaughter innocent people.'

Gigio raised a threatening finger.

'It's better to eliminate ten innocents than to spare one individual who may be dangerous to the cause. Dead men can do the Party no harm. You're a very poor Communist, as I've said before. In fact, you never were a good one. You're as weak as a snowball in Hell, I say; you're just a *bourgeois* in disguise!'

Brusco grew pale, and Peppone intervened.

'That's enough,' he said. 'Comrade Gigio has the right idea, and nobody can deny it. It's part of the groundwork of Communist philosophy. Communism gives us the goal at which to aim and democratic discussion must be confined to the choice of the quickest and surest ways to attain it.'

Gigio nodded his head in satisfaction, while Peppone continued: 'Once it's been decided that these persons are or may be dangerous to the cause and therefore we must eliminate them, the next thing is to work out the best method of elimination. Because if by our carelessness we were to allow a single reactionary to escape, then we should indeed be traitors to the Party. Is that clear?'

'Absolutely,' the others said in chorus. 'You're dead right.'

'There are six of us,' Peppone went on, 'and twenty names on the list, among them Filotti, who has a whole regiment in his house and a cache of arms in the cellar. If we were to attack these people one by one, at the first shot the rest would run away. We must call our forces together, and divide them up into twenty squads, each one equipped to deal with a particular objective.'

'Very good,' said Gigio.

'Good, my foot!' shouted Peppone. 'That's not the half of it! We need a twenty-first squad, equipped even better than the rest, to hold off the police. And mobile squads to cover the roads and the river. If a fellow rushes into action in the way you proposed, without proper precautions, running the risk of botching it completely, then he's not a good Communist, he's just a damned fool.'

It was Gigio's turn to pale now, and he bit his lip in anger while Peppone proceeded to give orders. Smilzo was to transmit word to the cell leaders in the outlying settlements, and these were to call their men together. A green rocket would give the signal to meet in appointed places, where Falchetto, Brusco, and Straziami would form the squads and assign the targets. A red rocket would bid them go into action. Smilzo went off on his motor-cycle, while Lungo, Brusco, Straziami, and Gigio discussed the composition of the squads.

'You must do a faultless job,' Peppone told them. 'I shall hold you personally responsible for its success.

Meanwhile, I'll see if the police are suspicious and find some way to put them off.'

Don Camillo, after waiting in vain for the lights to go on and the radio to resume its mumble, decided to get ready for bed. Suddenly he heard a knock at the door, and when he drew it open cautiously, he found Peppone before him.

'Get out of here in a hurry!' Peppone panted. 'Pack a bag and go! Put on an ordinary suit of clothes, take your boat and row down the river.'

Don Camillo stared at him with curiosity.

'Comrade Mayor, have you been drinking?'

'Hurry!' said Peppone. 'The People's Front has won, and the squads are getting ready. There's a list of people to be executed, and your name is the first one!'

Don Camillo bowed.

'An unexpected honour, Mr Mayor! But I must say I never expected you to be the sort of rascal that draws up lists for murder.'

'Don't be silly,' said Peppone impatiently. 'I don't want to murder anybody.'

'Well then?'

'Gigio, the lame fellow from Molinetto, came out with the list and secret Party orders.'

'You're the chief, Peppone. You could have sent him and his list to blazes.'

Peppone rubbed his perspiring face.

'You don't understand these things. The Party always has the last word, and he was speaking for the Party. If I'd stood out against him he'd have added my name to the list, above yours.'

'That's a good one! Comrade Peppone and the reactionary priest, Don Camillo, strung up together!'

'Hurry, will you?' Peppone repeated. 'You can afford to joke because you're all alone in the world, but I have a mother, a wife, a son and a whole lot of other dependants. Move fast if you want to save your skin!'

Don Camillo shook his head.

'Why should I be saved? What about the others?'

'I can't very well go to warn them, can I? You'll have to do that yourself. Drop in on one or two of them on your way to the river, and tell them to pass on the alarm. And they'd better look lively! Here, take down the names.'

'Very well,' said Don Camillo when he'd taken them down. 'I'll send the sexton's boy to call the Filotti family, and there are so many of them that they can take care of the rest. I'm staying here.'

'But you've got to go, I tell you!'

'This is my place, and I won't budge, even if Stalin comes in person.'

'You're crazy!' said Peppone, but before he could say anything else, there was a knock at the door and he had to run and hide in the next room.

The next arrival was Brusco, but he had barely time to say: 'Don Camillo, get out of here in a hurry!' before someone knocked at the door again. Brusco, too, ran to hide, and a minute later Lungo burst in.

'Don Camillo,' said Lungo, 'I've only just been able to sneak away for a minute. Things are hotting up, and you'd better get out. Here are the names of the other people you ought to take with you.'

And he rushed to hide, because there was another knock at the door. This time it was Straziami, as glum and pugnacious as ever. He had hardly stepped in, when Lungo, Brusco, and Peppone emerged to meet him.

'It's beginning to look like one of those old-fashioned comedies,' said Don Camillo, laughing. 'As soon as Gigio comes, the whole cast will be on the stage.'

'He's not coming,' muttered Peppone.

Then with a sigh, he slapped Brusco on the back.

'Notice anything?' he said reminiscently. 'Here we are again, the way we were up in the mountains in the old days of the Resistance. And we can still get along together.'

The others nodded.

'If Smilzo were only here the old guard would be complete,' sighed Peppone.

'He *is* here,' said Don Camillo. 'In fact, he was the first to come.'

'Good,' said Peppone approvingly. 'And now you'd better hustle.'

But Don Camillo was a stubborn man.

'I told you once that my place is here,' he said. 'I'm quite happy enough to know that you're not against me.'

Peppone lost patience. He twisted his hat about and then jammed it down on his head in the way that he did when he was ready to come to blows.

'You two take his shoulders, and I'll take his legs,' he ordered. 'It's too late to go by boat. We'll tie him to the seat of his cart and send him away. Straziami, go and harness the horse.'

But before they could raise their arms the lights went on, and they stood there, dazzled. A moment later the radio began to mumble. 'Here are the results of the election of Deputies to Parliament, with 41,000 out of 41,168 electoral districts heard from: Christian Democrats, 12,000,257 votes; People's Front, 7,547,468 ...'

They all listened in silence until the announcement was over. Then Peppone looked gloomily at Don Camillo.

'Some weeds are so tough that they overrun everything,' he said angrily. 'You had a lucky escape, that's all I can say.'

'You had a lucky escape yourself,' Don Camillo answered calmly, 'for which God be praised.'

One man didn't escape and that was Gigio. He was

proudly waiting for orders to set off the green rocket and, instead, he got a volley of kicks that left him black and blue all over.

26 · BACK TO 1922

IN the village and its surroundings there were quite a lot of people who started as early as February to lay aside money for the pre-Lenten Carnival. There were twelve rival clubs, five in the village and seven in the countryside, and every Saturday the members contributed part of their pay to the decoration of the floats which each one entered in the parade. In short, the brief Carnival season was a very important affair.

The floats came into being bit by bit in farmyards scattered over the plain. Each club chose the farmyard most suitable for the purpose and with poles, sticks, reed mats and blinds, strips of canvas and tarred paper built a shed which housed the construction. Only members of the club were allowed to look in until the great day came. Then the shed was joyfully torn down and the float emerged, for all the world like a chick newly hatched from the shell. There were sizeable prizes to be won, and individual floats and costumed figures came from nearby townships and even from the city. For three whole days the village was crowded.

The Carnival was a serious affair, not only because it drew so many people in a spending mood to the village, but also because it brought with it a complete truce to all political activities. For this reason Don Camillo never made it the butt of any of his sermons.

'Lord,' he explained to Christ over the main altar, 'we've come to a point where men behave themselves only when they're silly. Let's allow them their fun: *Semel in anno licet insanire.*'

As for Mayor Peppone, he frowned upon the Carnival because it irritated him to see that men couldn't pull together for any cause other than a frivolous one.

'They'll all come across with the money to decorate one of those stupid floats,' he protested. 'But just try to put over something worth while, such as the People's Revolution, and every last one of them is a skinflint.'

Peppone spoke against the Carnival for six months of the year. For the other six months he worked overtime organizing the parade and helping to build his own club's float. Incidentally, he put up considerable money. And if a local float failed to win the first prize, he took it as a personal insult.

That year everything smiled upon the Carnival, because it came in a period of exceptionally fine weather and people came from far and wide to see it. Competing floats and wearers of fancy dress arrived from a widespread area, and no one had ever witnessed so long a parade, which as usual wound its way around the village three times. From his post in the grandstand Peppone looked down at the first round with general satisfaction, finding it worthy of the population gathered in such large numbers to acclaim it. As a result his deportment seemed to be modelled upon that of the Lord Mayor of London.

When the parade came around for the second time, he began to look more closely at the various entries in order to determine whether those of the village were likely to carry away the first prize, or at least the second, third, fourth, and fifth prizes, In other words, he was transformed from Lord Mayor of London into mayor of his own town. And among the single competitors for a fancy-dress prize his eyes fell upon a Red Indian riding a motor-cycle. After the fellow had gone by, he wondered exactly what had drawn his attention, for the costume had nothing extraordinary about it, being composed chiefly of a big cardboard nose and a band of chicken feathers around the head. He concluded that it must have reminded him of something from times gone by, and sure enough, it came to him in a flash that it was the poster figure that used to advertise 'Indian Motor-cycles'.

During the third round Peppone ascertained that there was indeed a basis for his conclusion. This was the 'Indian Motor-cycle' figure, and no mistake about it. Only the figure wasn't riding an 'Indian' at all; he was astride an old B.S.A. model. Where motor-cycles and their engines were concerned, Peppone was like one of those musical quiz experts, who no sooner hear a few notes from a piece than they can tell you its title and composer. And there was a further reason why he could make no mistake: this particular motor-cycle had been in his hands for repairs at least a hundred times. Only one question remained in Peppone's mind: Who was riding in Indian costume on Dario Camoni's old B.S.A.?

He left the grandstand, having momentarily lost all interest in the parade. This was a matter that had nothing to do with the mayoralty; it was of a strictly private character. He made his way with difficulty through the crowd, trying to keep up with the Indian, and during a brief pause, the latter turned his head and looked at him. Peppone's doubts vanished. The rider of Dario Camoni's old B.S.A. was Dario Camoni. Even behind a cardboard mask, those were unmistakably his eyes.

Peppone continued to follow the parade, step by step, and nothing in the world could have stopped his implacable *Panzer* pursuit. When the parade had gone around for the third time it drew up in the open space between the village and the river and disbanded. There was such an array of floats, lorries, and farm wagons that the Indian could not possibly escape. The only opening in the crowd was on to the street that had led them away from the central square. He was aware that Peppone had been following him and did not hesitate to turn around in this direction, even at the risk of running down a pedestrian. But after he had gone a few yards an enormous float blocked the street and he had to dart into an alley on the right, with Peppone practically panting down his neck from behind.

The smaller square in front of the church was deserted, and the redskin sped up the alley with this destination in view. A few seconds later, he braked his machine abruptly in order not to run down Don Camillo, who was smoking a cigar butt in front of the rectory. Once upon a time this alley had made a right-angle turn just in front of the rectory and gone into the road leading to the river, but for the last ten years it had been blocked off.

Don Camillo was stunned by the abruptness of the motor-cycle's arrival. His impulse was to grab the fellow by the chest and knock his head against the wall for his reckless folly. But he was too late. The motor-cyclist had dropped his machine on the street and dashed through the rectory's open door. A second later Peppone rushed upon the scene, and without so much as a glance at the priest, followed the fugtitive's example. But Don Camillo's powerful body stood in the way.

'What the devil?' Don Camillo shouted. 'What in the world are you doing? First an Indian nearly runs me down with a motor-cycle and then a mayor bumps into me on foot. Is it all part of some symbolical charade?'

'Look, you've got to let me in,' panted Peppone, reluctantly drawing back. 'I have a score to settle with Dario Camoni.'

'Camoni? How does he come into the picture?'

'That Indian is Camoni!' said Peppone between clenched teeth.

Don Camillo pushed Peppone back, went into the rectory and fastened the door behind him with a chain. The Indian was sitting in the study, and the first thing Don Camillo did was to pull off his cardboard nose.

'Well, it's me, all right,' said the Indian, rising from his chair. 'What are you going to do about it?'

Don Camillo sat down at his desk and relighted his cigar.

'Nothing at all,' he answered, after he had blown several puffs of smoke into the air. 'But you'd be better off if you really were an Indian.'

Back in 1922 the river country of the little world was still in a state of political ferment, even although elsewhere the Fascists had consolidated their governmental position. The land had something to do with it, and so did the boiling-point of its people. Dario Camoni was seventeen years old, and he wanted to make up for the time when he was too young to take part in the Black-versus-Red battle. In 1919, when he was a mere fourteen years old, some Reds had beaten up his father for refusing to take part in a farm labour strike, right in front of his eyes. This explains, among other things, why three years later Dario was still in a combative mood, and ready to beat up any stray Red he could find for revenge.

Dario Camoni was a husky boy, and above all a hot-headed one. When he went into action his eyes blazed in a way that was more convincing than any amount of words. Peppone was several years older and stood head and shoulders above him, but those cursed eyes caused him to steer clear. One evening when Peppone was talking to his girl on the bridge in front of her house, Dario Camoni rode up on a motor-cycle.

'Sorry to intrude,' he said, 'but I've been given a job to do.'

He took a glass and a bottle out of his pocket and proceeded to empty the contents of the bottle into the glass.

'The doctor says you have indigestion and a little laxative will do you good,' he continued, advancing with the full glass in one hand and his other hand grasping a hard object in his pocket. 'My advice to you is to take your medicine, because some of this castor oil dripped on to my revolver and I don't want the trigger to slip in my fingers. If the dose is too strong for you, you can share it with your girl. I'm going to count to three. One ... two ...'

Peppone took the glass and drained it to the last drop.

'Good for you!' said Dario Camoni, mounting his motor-cycle. 'Be careful not to step on certain people's toes, or you may get something worse next time.'

Although Peppone had managed to drink the castor oil, a form of punishment which the Fascists had brought into style, he could not swallow the insult, which was all the more grave because Dario had humiliated him in front of his girl. As it happened, he married the girl later on, but that made it worse rather than better. Every time that he raised his voice at home his wife taunted him:

'If the fellow who gave you the dose of castor oil that night were here, you wouldn't be up on such a high horse, would you?'

No, Peppone had never forgotten this dirty trick, and neither, for that matter, had Don Camillo. In that far-away 1922, Don Camillo was a greenhorn priest, just out of the seminary, but he was nobody's fool and preached a sermon against violence in general, and in particular against the bullies who were going around forcing unsavoury drinks upon other people. For this reason, one night he was called downstairs because someone was fatally ill and needed Extreme Unction. When he came down, there was Dario Camoni, with a Mauser in one hand and a glass of castor oil in the other.

'You're the one that needs the oil, Father, even if it's unholy. This will make your motor hum. And because I owe you particular respect as a member of the clergy, I'll count to four instead of to three.'

And Don Camillo drank his ration down.

'There, Father,' said Dario Camoni, 'you'll see how much more clearly your brain will function tomorrow. And if you really want to be reduced to a condition where you'll need holy oil rather than unholy, just go on sticking your nose into our business.'

'The church's business extends to everything that concerns good Christian people,' objected Don Camillo.

'If we'd used Christian behaviour towards the Reds, your church would be a Red headquarters and seat of the Consumer's Co-operative today! Anyhow, whenever you need to change the oil in your motor, just whistle!'

Like Peppone, Don Camillo had found it easier to swallow the oil than the insult.

'Lord,' he said several times to Christ over the altar. 'If he'd beaten me up, it would be different. But castor oil is too much. You can kill a priest, but you have no right to make him ridiculous with a dose of castor oil!'

Years went by, and Dario Camoni remained an active Fascist as long as there was strong-arm work to be done. Then he retired from politics altogether. But he had oiled and beaten up too many people in his time to be forgotten. When the régime was overturned, in 1945, he found things too hot for him and went away. And Peppone sent word after him to say that if he showed his face in the village it would be at the risk of his skin. More years passed, without news of Dario Camoni. And now he had returned, in the disguise of a Red Indian.

'I'd like to know what got into your head to think up something like this,' Don Camillo said to Dario Camoni.

'I've been away from home for six years,' murmured the Indian, 'and wanted like anything to come back. The only way I could do it was in disguise. Seems to me it wasn't such a bad idea.'

'Poor Camoni!' Don Camillo said with a sigh. 'You're so comical in your Indian dress that I'm inclined to be sorry for you. An Indian on a motor-cycle, who takes refuge in the priest's house from a mayor who is chasing him on foot. It's almost as melodramatic as the comics. Well, you may as well take it easy. You're almost a hundred per cent safe. If there weren't that glass of castor oil between us, I'd say a hundred per cent with no reservations.'

'Is that silly business still on your mind?' asked the Indian, who was still panting from the chase. 'That was thirty years ago and childish.'

Don Camillo was about to embark upon a long harangue when the study door swung open and Peppone appeared on the scene.

'Excuse me, Father, for coming through the window,' he said, 'but I had no other choice, since I couldn't come through the door.'

The Indian had leaped to his feet, for the expression on Peppone's face wasn't exactly pretty. Moreover, Peppone had an iron bar in his hand and looked as if he intended to put it to use. Don Camillo stepped between them.

'Don't let's have a tragedy in the middle of the Carnival,' he interposed. 'We must all be calm.'

'I'm perfectly calm,' said Peppone, 'and I have no intention of causing a tragedy. I have a job to do, that's all.'

He took two glasses out of one pocket, then, without taking his eyes off the Indian, a bottle out of the other and divided its contents between them.

'There,' he said, standing back against the door. 'The doctor says you have indigestion and a little laxative will do you good. Hurry up, because the oil has greased my iron bar and I'm afraid it may slip and fall on to your head. Drink down both glassfuls, one to my health and the other to the health of Don Camillo. I'm happy to pay my respects to him in this way.'

The Indian turned pale as he backed up against the wall, and Peppone was truly fear-inspiring.

'Drink them down, I tell you!' he shouted, raising the iron bar.

'No, I won't,' answered the Indian.

Peppone rushed forward and grabbed him by the neck.

'I'll make you drink!' he shouted.

But the Indian's neck and face were covered with grease-paint and he managed to free himself. He leaped behind the table, and as Peppone and Don Camillo noticed too late for their own good, he took down the shotgun hanging on the wall and pointed it straight at Peppone.

'Don't do anything crazy,' shouted Don Camillo, drawing over to one side, 'that thing is loaded.'

The Indian advanced on his enemy.

'Throw down that bar,' he said sternly, and his eyes were as blazing as they had been thirty years before. Peppone and Don Camillo both remembered them distinctly, and knew that Dario Camoni was quite capable of shooting. Peppone let the bar fall to the floor.

'Now *you* drink,' the Indian said between clenched teeth to Peppone. 'I'll count to three. One ... two ...'

Yes, he had the same wild eyes and the same voice as long ago. Peppone gulped down the contents of one of the glasses.

'And now go back where you came from,' the Indian commanded.

Peppone went away, and the Indian barred the study door.

'He can send his police if he wants to,' he said, 'but if I'm killed, I won't go to Hell alone.'

Don Camillo relit his cigar.

'That's enough of your horseplay,' he said quietly. 'Put down that gun and go away.'

'Go away yourself,' said the Indian coldly. 'I'm waiting for them here.'

'Very unwise, Redskin,' said the priest. 'I don't believe the palefaces will come, but if they do, how can you defend yourself with an empty gun?'

'That's an old joke and a poor one,' laughed the Indian. 'I wasn't born yesterday, for your information!'

Don Camillo went to sit down on the other side of the room.

'Just look and see,' he suggested.

The suspicious Camoni peered into the gun and his face whitened. The gun was not loaded.

'Put the gun down,' said Don Camillo quietly; 'take off your costume, leave the rectory on the garden side and cut through the fields. If you hurry, you'll catch the bus at Fontanile. I'll put your motor-cycle in safe-keeping, and you can either let me know where to send it or else come and fetch it in person.'

The Indian laid the gun on the desk.

'No use looking for the cartridges,' Don Camillo told him. He had put on his glasses and was reading the paper. 'The cartridges are in the cupboard and the key to the cupboard is in my pocket. I warn you that unless you get out of here in double-quick time, I'll be reminded of that drink you pressed upon me long ago.'

The Indian tore off the remains of his costume and wiped the grease-paint off his face. He took a cap out of his pocket and jammed it down over his head. Dario Camoni started to leave the room, but he lingered at the door and turned hesitantly around.

'Let's even the score,' he said, and picking up the second glass of castor oil, he drained it.

'Quits?' he said interrogatively.

'Quits,' answered Don Camillo, without even raising his head.

And the Indian disappeared.

Peppone came back later, looking green around the gills.

'I hope you won't sink so low as to go around telling what happened to me,' he said gloomily.

'I should say not,' Don Camillo answered with a sigh. 'You had one glass, but that wretch made me drink the other.'

'Has he gone away?' asked Peppone, sitting down.

'Gone with the wind.'

Peppone stared at the floor and said nothing.

'Well, what can I say?' he finally mumbled. 'It was a little like going back to the time when we were young, thirty years ago ...'

'True enough,' said Don Camillo. 'That Indian brought back a bit of our youth.'

Peppone started to relapse into anger.

'Easy there, Peppone,' Don Camillo advised him. 'You don't want to endanger the dignity of your office.'

Peppone went cautiously home, and Don Camillo made a report to the Crucified Christ over the altar.

'Lord,' he explained, 'what else could I do? If I'd told Peppone the gun wasn't loaded he'd have killed the other fellow for sure. Those Camonis are too pig-headed to ever give in. As things are, there was no violence, and the Indian had a dose of oil, which You must chalk up to his credit. And by sacrificing my personal pride, I managed not to humiliate Peppone.'

'Don Camillo,' Christ answered, 'when the Indian told Peppone to drink the oil, you knew the gun wasn't loaded and you could perfectly well have stepped in.'

'Lord,' said Don Camillo, throwing out his arms in resignation, 'what if Peppone had found out that the gun wasn't loaded and failed to get that healthy drink?'

'Don Camillo,' Christ said severely, 'I ought to prescribe a drink of the same kind for you!'

It seems that as Don Camillo left the church he was muttering something to the effect that only Fascists could order any such prescription. But this is not altogether certain. In any case, when he hung the shotgun up on the wall, he placed the Indian bonnet as a trophy beside it, and every time he looked at it he reflected that there is perfectly good hunting to be found without benefit of a gun.